Murder Mamas

Murder Mamas

Ashley & JaQuavis

www.urbanbooks.net

Urban Books, LLC
78 East Industry Court
Deer Park, NY 11729

ISBN 13: 978-1-60162-500-7
ISBN 10: 1-60162-500-6

First Printing October 2011
Printed in the United States of America

20 19 18 17 16 15 14 13

Distributed by Kensington Publishing Corp.
Submit Wholesale Orders to:
Kensington Publishing Corp.
C/O Penguin Group (USA) Inc.
Attention: Order Processing
405 Murray Hill Parkway
East Rutherford, NJ 07073-2316
Phone: 1-800-526-0275
Fax: 1-800-227-9604

Prologue

Case slowly walked back and forth across the front of the spacious church. Both hands were behind his back as he wore Armani slacks, shirt, and a tie. His strong posture and piercing eyes symbolized power, and the entire city felt it. He took his time, knowing that he wanted to choose his words wisely.

The first three rows of the pews were filled with important guests, listening to the man who had ruled over the streets for more than a decade. He called a meeting at one of the city's abandoned buildings that once was a church. Case looked at his audience, many of whom were some of the head hustlers in the city, and they remained silent as they listened closely to the man who had the floor.

Case's drug operation had suffered a big blow because of the recent narcotics crackdown led by Macy Sigel, the city's mayor. Macy was the creator of a newly formed task force that focused on the drug problem in the inner city. This put a direct strain on Case's cash flow. He decided to call a meeting and clear up all debt and beefs in the streets because he was about to make a power move. He was about to murk the mayor and wanted the streets behind him when he did it.

"You are all here today because I chose you to be here. In some shape or form, every one of you have gone against the grain. Some of you failed to pay me my twenty percent, some of you owe me money, and some of you, well, some of you I just don't like," Case said as he stood before the men, staring at each individual in the eye.

It was a moment of silence in the room, and all that was heard was the breathing of the men. The smell of fear was in the air. Case smiled as he was overcome with the buzz that goes along with having power. It was like a natural high being a man with such influence, and he enjoyed the view from the top as he looked down at the others before him.

"Anybody have anything to say?" Case asked sarcastically. In actuality, no one could say anything because duct tape covered their mouths, stifling them, while their hands and feet were bound.

Case looked over to his right, where his henchman stood guard. Case gave him a signal, and the henchman picked up the can of gas that sat at his feet and began to go up and down the aisle, pouring gasoline over the heads and bodies of the hustlers in attendance.

"I told y'all muthafuckas, do not fuck me! Now look at you," Case said as he lit a cigar. He headed down the aisle, and his henchman followed.

The moans and pleas fell on deaf ears, as Case wanted to set an example for the whole city. Business had slowed up, and he had to tighten down on his organization and restore order in the streets. Case didn't like to be a bad guy, but he was so good at it.

He waited for his henchman to empty the can and join him. He then took a pull of the cigar and tossed it into the aisle. Case instantly sent the place and its patrons up in flames.

Case's henchman opened the car door for him and commented on the situation. "This guy Macy Sigel is fucking up the whole organization. We got to do something to this nigga. It's going to be hard to touch the mayor though. He constantly has his people around him."

Case looked down at his watch and saw that he only had thirty minutes to get to the state penitentiary, where he had unfinished business to attend to. "I know how I can get to this nigga. I have to call an old friend up. She owes me a favor. I know exactly where I can find her, too," Case stated surely.

Case sat in the back seat of his Maybach as his henchman guided the luxury car off the avenue. They were on their way to witness the death of a Murder Mama.

Thump . . . Thump.
Thump . . . Thump.
Thump . . . Thump.

Aries' heartbeat was deafening as her chest heaved up and down. She could hardly breathe as she moved through the short line. There were about fifteen people in attendance. Undoubtedly, she was the only supporter in the room. She could not believe that things had come to this point, and her hands shook violently as she signed in, putting her John Hancock on the witness log.

A member of the most notorious Murder Mama crew, she had committed many sins. As a murderer for hire, she had learned long ago to bury her emotions deep inside of her. Fear was something that she had never allowed herself to feel, but as she got processed through the prison system, the dormant emotion surfaced to the top. She had no idea what to expect, and as she was searched, her old instincts kicked in. Her eyes scanned the room thoroughly, looking into the eyes of the prison guards. She half expected them to detain her at any moment. She deserved a thousand years for the crimes that she had under her belt, and she was wary about putting herself in the position to be caught.

As badly as she wanted to skip out, she knew that this was one event that she had to be a part of. It was only fair. Her friends had been there for her through thick and thin. They had come up together and as fate had taken its course, they had fallen together as well. Her attendance was mandatory, and she took a deep breath to calm her nerves as she tried to get through the ordeal.

The guards escorted the small group to a room with rowed seating, and Aries quickly reserved one in the front row, dead center. Looking through the thick glass window before her, she saw the contraption that had ended many more lives than she ever could. She felt sick to her stomach as she thought about what was about to occur. As badly as she wanted to do something to stop what was about to happen, it was out of her hands. The only thing that she could do was witness an execution.

Her heart ached as she watched her friend Robyn enter the room. Shackles tightly bound her hands and feet. The navy prison-issued jumpsuit she wore swallowed her slim frame. Aries' chest caved in from pure emotion as she felt tears sting her eyes. They were about to kill her girl, her Murder Mama, signifying the end of their reign over the underworld's murder game.

Around her, the family members of those Robyn had bodied cried and thanked God for justice, but there was nothing just about it. Robyn was like her sister, and the state was about to put her down like a rabid dog.

The entire Murder Mama crew had been decimated, and although Aries had felt loss before, this one hurt the most. Not because she loved Robyn more, but because Robyn wasn't dying a free woman. Aries knew that if Robyn had her way, she would have preferred to bleed out in the streets while doing what she did best. This wasn't how any of them had envisioned their end. This was no storybook or no hood legend myth. The streets couldn't glorify this. Robyn had been caught and a jury of her peers had found her guilty; another man had sentenced her to die.

Karma had come full circle for Robyn, and as Aries locked eyes with her dear friend, she felt her pain. Aries studied Robyn's features and noticed how placid, how serene she looked. She wanted to nod at her, to blow her a kiss, or to do something to acknowledge her, but they both knew that any communication could put Aries at risk.

The police had questioned Robyn for years trying to get her to give up the other member of the notorious Murder Mamas crew. The state had even presented her with a deal. If Robyn had talked, she wouldn't be dying today; but she had stood tall and carried the sentence for them both. She was dying for Aries and on behalf of her loyalty to the rest of her deceased crew. Loyalty and their love for one another was all they had. Robyn refused to betray that. Aries closed her eyes and spoke to God.

Please take care of my friend, God. Please look after her. Make it painless and quick. Forgive her for the things that we've done. She's held the burden of enough blame. Hold me accountable for the rest.

Aries lifted her head and watched helplessly as the prison guards strapped Robyn down on the gurney; then a man in a white doctor's coat inserted an IV into the vein on the back of her hand. Aries cringed with worry, but she never stopped looking Robyn in the eyes. She put her arm on the armrest of her chair and brought her hand to her face to lean on it. She discreetly kissed the tattoo on her wrist that read, MURDER MAMAS. She knew that Robyn would know that the gesture was meant for her.

A priest came into the room and opened a Bible, quoting scripture out of respect. When he was done he asked, "Do you have any last words?"

Tears finally emerged from Robyn's eyes as a moment of absolution came over her. Aries, unable to contain herself any longer, shivered as her cold tears rolled down her cheeks. She was stricken with guilt and filled with admiration all at the same time.

"I love you, Murder Mama. Live. Live for the rest of us who no longer can. We love you," Robyn said while staring Aries directly in the eyes.

The doctor flipped a switch, and Aries watched in horror as the lethal combination of medicines traveled through the plastic tubes. It all happened in slow motion, and Aries felt as if her heart would explode as grief paralyzed her. When the concoction reached Robyn's IV, Aries couldn't stop the sob from escaping her lips. She put her hand to her mouth to stop herself from crying aloud, but her eyes never left Robyn's. It was the only way for them to connect in Robyn's final moments.

Robyn held on as long as she could, but as the poison entered her system, she slowly faded. She fought it as long as she could, but the overwhelming sleepiness plagued her, and her eyelids betrayed her as they began to close.

The doctor monitored Robyn's pulse and heartbeat until she flatlined on the screen. He looked at the clock and announced, "Time of death, 7:07 P.M."

Aries lowered her head and whispered, "Rest in peace."

It was the most pain she had ever felt and the worst day of her life.

She arose from her seat and stormed out of the room, searching for the nearest exit. It suddenly felt as if there were no air in the room. "I have to get out of here," she whispered as she emerged out of the building and the sunlight beamed down on her.

The contents of her stomach erupted, and she keeled over as she vomited onto the pavement. Although death had been her occupation, seeing a person she loved be put down rocked her entire world. She quickly gathered herself and wiped her mouth with the back of her hand before leaving the prison behind. She vowed that she would never step foot inside one again.

She picked up her cell phone and noticed that she had three missed calls. She dialed the numbers back and put the phone on speakerphone as she put distance between herself and the barbaric prison.

"Rachel, hey, baby. I've been calling you all morning," her husband, Prince, said.

"Hey, honey. I'm sorry. I had to take my mother to the hospital this morning. Her blood pressure is out of control, and she just isn't in good spirits. Her health is fading, and the doctor was trying to explain a few things to me. I couldn't answer for you," she replied, the lie slipping off so easily that even she believed it.

She had become an expert at lying during the five years that she had been in hiding. Her real mother had been dead for so long that Aries rarely ever thought of her.

After Robyn's arrest, Aries had been forced to change her entire life. Her identity, her look, even her accent had to be reinvented. Aries now lived as Rachel Coleman, housewife and mother. Her world was so far removed from the tyranny that she sometimes couldn't believe she had ever lived so ruthlessly.

Days like this were a reminder of what she used to be. She was a killer and she was a part of a murder-for-hire team whose names would ring bells in the streets for years to come; but to Prince Coleman she was just Rachel, his lovely wife. He had no idea who he was sleeping next to at night.

"When should Tre and I expect you?" he asked.

"I'm coming home tomorrow. I did what I came here to do. It's been five years since I left here, and now I remember why I've stayed away for so long. I've had enough of this city. Everything is dead to me here. I wouldn't care if I never came back," she replied.

Aries wrapped the apron around her summer dress and pulled up her long hair as she prepared her family's breakfast. After Robyn's execution, she had caught a late flight back to her home in Barbados. Going back had sparked a lot of bad memories for her. Ever since she saw the drugs enter Robyn's system, she had been having visions of blood on her hands. Her conscience was playing tricks on her, and deep regret had begun to fill her soul as she thought of all the reckless murders she had taken part in. She could have easily been in Robyn's shoes.

The red tint that stained her hands was only visible to Aries. She felt as if she were losing her mind, and as a tear slipped from her eye, she rushed to the stainless steel sink. She rubbed her hands together vigorously under the cold, flowing water and took deep breaths as she closed her eyes. *It's not real. You don't live that life anymore. Forgive yourself,* she thought.

When her nerves had settled and her pulse had slowed, she slowly opened her eyes. She sighed in relief as she turned off the faucet and went back to cooking for her family.

When she had first exited the game, her paranoia had almost driven her crazy. Everyone was somebody to her—somebody who wanted to see her dead. The mailman, the lady cashier at the local market, even her next door neighbor: She had suspected them all of being out to get her. It had taken her five long years to transition into a normal lifestyle, and she refused to allow the corruption of L.A. to set her back in her old ways.

"Mama!"

The tiny voice behind her made her smile, and she turned to greet her three-year-old son. He stood in front of her wearing Batman pajamas and a huge smile. He ran toward her at full speed and leapt into her open arms.

"Hey, mama's baby. Oh my goodness, I missed you," she whispered as she snuggled his neck and gave him a million kisses all over his face.

"I missed you too," her son replied. Seeing his innocent face instantly turned her mood around and her spirits went from low to high.

Aries scooped him up in her arms and said, "Let's go wake your daddy."

She carried her son up to her bedroom, and they both hopped on top of Prince. He lazily opened his eyes as he pulled her under the covers.

"Hey, baby, what are you doing here? I thought I was supposed to pick you up from the airport after I left the office," he said as he wiped the sleep from his eyes and adjusted the hard-on in his linen pajama pants.

"I flew back early. I wanted to see my two men off this morning," she said sweetly. One would have never known that this island beauty had a sinister past.

He cuddled with his wife and son, then discreetly reached in between her legs, fondling her juicy clit.

"Hmm-hmm, boy. Don't even try it," she said with a seductive smile. "You know your son is not having that."

He put his hand over his face and shook his head with a knowing smile. "I swear that boy has a radar or something. A nigga can't get no pussy while he is awake," Prince commented playfully.

Their son hopped up and down at the end of the mattress, and Aries chuckled softly. "I made you two breakfast. We'll be downstairs waiting on you," she announced before grabbing her son's hand and walking out of the room.

Her life now was so simple, and although at times it felt slow, she had to remind herself that it didn't carry the same risks as the one she used to lead. She had left the streets alone a long time ago, and she vowed that nothing would ever pull her back in. The allure of it all wasn't worth it anymore. When she was young and reckless, it all seemed like a big adventure, but now, at the age of thirty, she just wanted peace.

It had been five years since her finger had wrapped around a trigger, and she had made a whole new life for herself. In her native country of Barbados, she lived happily and in tranquility. She had told herself that she would never return to the States, but missing Robyn's execution was not an option. The trip had sparked bad memories for her, but as she catered to her family's needs, she shook them off.

Prince joined his wife and son in the kitchen, and Aries admired his handsome appearance. She walked toward him and handed him a plate of food then grabbed his tie and pulled him into her for a kiss. Watching her family do something as simple as enjoying the morning breeze brought pure joy to her heart. After the things her eyes had seen, she was fortunate to live such a tame life. She was the last person who deserved a happy ending, but somehow she had wound up with one.

Aries played the role to perfection as she saw her husband off to work, standing in the doorway with her child in her arms as she waved good-bye. By the time his black S-Class disappeared from sight, Tre was dozing off on her shoulder. She closed the door and put him down in his bed.

DING DONG!

She stood up and shook her head, knowing that Prince had forgotten his briefcase once again. He was so unorganized that she could not understand how he was one of the most prominent accountants in the country. But his client list alone told of his status. She went into his office to retrieve his briefcase, but when she looked behind his desk, it was nowhere to be found. She frowned and looked around in confusion. Prince always kept his briefcase in the same place.

DING DONG!

The doorbell sounded off again, and she ran down the stairs to answer the door. "I was going to bring it to you, but—"

Her words stopped when she lifted her head and met eyes with the man who stood before her. Fear paralyzed her, and she felt as if she couldn't breathe. Her killer instincts kicked back in as her hand immediately shot to her waistline, but unfortunately her days of pistol toting were long gone.

Tears filled her eyes as she realized she was about to be murdered while her son slept soundly upstairs. She had known that her past would come back to haunt her one day. She stiffened her jaw and held her head up, preparing to die the Murder Mama way, proud and unflinching.

As her son began crying she winced, knowing that the man before her had no mercy on children. That's when she broke down. It was in that moment that regret filled her heart and she thought back to the very first day that she had crossed this man, wishing that she could take it all back. . . .

Chapter One

Five years earlier

Robyn and Aries looked at the stacks of hundred and fifty dollar bills scattered all over the red-top pool table. Case slowly circled the table and finished dumping the cash out of the Gucci duffle bag. Casey James, also known as Case, was well over six foot, dark as tar, and as ruthless as they came. Cocaine was the name of the game, and he was the head of the black market of Los Angeles. He was putting his money where his mouth was and was laying out a million dollars of dirty money for the kidnapping of a federal judge's daughter. Case's younger brother was caught with twenty kilos of cocaine a few months back, and his fate rested on the shoulders of the jury and a known racist judge.

"There you go, ladies. One million dollars," he said as he rested both of his hands on the rim of the pool table and leaned over the pile of money. Aries and Robyn smiled as they looked at the abundance of bills.

"Hold on. Give us a second," Robyn said as she stepped to the side to have a sidebar with Aries.

"That's a lot of money right there, Aries," Robyn said as she glanced back at the table.

"I know. But is it worth it?" Aries asked in her heavy island accent as she thought about what task was at hand. Murder was one thing, but to be asked to kidnap someone was a totally different ball game.

"I say go for it," Robyn said as she thought about the money that they would be leaving on the table if they turned the offer down.

"Fuck it. Let's do it," Aries said, not caring about the degree of difficulty the job required. She was ready to get paid and willing to go to the extreme to achieve her big payday. They both went to the table, and Case saw the greed in their eyes.

"Deal," Aries said as she grabbed the bag and began to stuff the money back inside of it. "We get to keep the bag, right?" Aries said as she gave him a small smirk.

Case smiled back and nodded his head. If it were not for business, he would have pushed up on Aries. She reminded him of Rihanna, and her accent was sexy to him. He quickly dismissed the notion, but not before looking at her slim frame and round assets.

He was glad that he had gotten plugged in with the infamous Murder Mamas. For a long time, he thought they were a myth, but he quickly was made a believer when they showed up to his spot. After he put the word on the streets that he was looking for them, it did not take them long to find him. He knew that they were the best in the business, and the job he requested needed to be done by the best.

"Okay, look. I've already done my homework on this racist prick," Case said as he walked over to his desk that sat in the back of the room and reached into his desk. He pulled out a legal-sized envelope and walked back to them. "He lives just outside of the city and has a wife and daughter," he said as he tossed the pictures onto the pool table. There were photos of the fifty-something Caucasian judge kissing his wife and then a picture of him getting into his Benz.

"He leaves for work every morning at seven-fifteen sharp, and the kid gets on the bus at seven o'clock. You guys should catch him coming out and force him back into the house. Don't play with this mu'fucka! Establish from the beginning that you guys are willing to kill if not listened to. What I need is for you to enter the home, tie up his wife in front of him, and let him know what it is. I want him to know that if my brother doesn't get a verdict in our favor, it's curtains. His wife will be knocked off," Case said, meaning every word of it.

He needed someone who wasn't afraid to pull the trigger if needed, and that's exactly why he called on the best in the business. He wasn't taking any chances and resting the fate of his brother in a racist judge's hands. His brother's trial was a no-jury trial because of the notoriety of his crew. The court didn't want to worry about jury tampering, but Case was a step ahead of them. He was going straight to the source with no reservations.

"Say no more," Aries said as she tossed the bag over her shoulders.

Case then handed the envelope to Robyn, who had a key to the judge's house, his address, and the photos of his wife and kid. They were given all the tools to make it happen smoothly; now the only thing left to do was to execute.

Case watched as the ladies exited through the back door and faded into the black. He smiled while moving the toothpick around in his mouth. He felt good about the money he had spent. The only thing he would have to do at that point was to wait.

"What the fuck?" Aries whispered under her breath as she glanced at her watch. She noticed that it was 7:30 and Robyn was running late. She was supposed to meet her at the Starbucks around the corner from the judge's home. Aries had been calling Robyn, but her phone kept going to voice mail. "Come on, gal," Aries said, her accent being more evident because she was getting upset.

Just as she picked up her phone to call Robyn, she pulled up right next to her. Robyn parked and jumped into the tinted sedan with Aries. Their plan was to catch the judge just before he went out.

"Where have chu been? I've been calling chu all morning," Aries said as she put her hands up in frustration.

"I got pulled over! What was I supposed to say? 'Hey, officer, can you hurry up so I can go kidnap a federal judge's wife?'" Robyn said sarcastically.

"We have to hurry up and hope he's running late," Aries said as she pulled off and headed toward the judge's suburb. Aries pushed the black sedan, and when they finally reached the suburb, they saw the judge's Benz whizzing past them.

"Fuck! There he goes!' Robyn said as she hit the dashboard. It was the day scheduled that the verdict would be delivered, so they had to act quickly.

"Okay . . . Okay. Let's go after him," Aries suggested as she clenched her jaws in frustration.

"No, we can't! Look where we are. The police will be on our ass before he gets his out the car. We have to follow through as planned. Let's tie up the bitch, and then you will have to go to the courthouse and get to him somehow to let him know what's going down. I will put his wife on the phone so he knows that it's not a game," Robyn said as she put the plan together on the fly.

"Okay, okay. That sounds good. Let's go," Aries said as she continued to the house.

They had a key to the house, so gaining entry wouldn't be a problem. The two ladies were dressed professionally, so it wouldn't throw any red flags up with the nosey neighbors, and also they wore wigs to hide their true hair color. They looked more like real estate agents than hired killers.

They both stepped out of the car with clipboards in hand. They approached the door, and Aries slid the key in the door while Robyn looked around to see if the coast was clear.

Aries clicked over the lock and entered the luxurious house. The smell of bacon and eggs filled the air as they entered the home. They both stuffed the clipboards into the oversized bag that Robyn carried and pulled out the nine millimeters.

"Hey, honey! Is that you?" a voice came in from the kitchen. Robyn and Aries proceeded into the kitchen, and a blond Caucasian woman was over the stove scrambling eggs. She never saw it coming.

"Hon . . ." she began to say as she turned around. She thought she was about to see her husband walking in because he had forgot something like he always did. However, two guns were pointed directly at her.

"Aghhh!" the lady yelled in sheer terror as she dropped the spatula and froze in fear.

"Shut up, bitch. Listen to what I say and nobody will get hurt," Robyn ordered as she approached the lady and grabbed her by the back of her neck. She guided her into the living room and made her sit on the couch.

Aries grabbed the bag that Robyn had placed on the floor and began to grab the ties and duct tape from it. As soon as the lady sat down, Aries was already beginning to tie her up, while Robyn pointed the gun to her head. The lady cried hysterically as her limbs shook uncontrollably.

"You got this," Aries said as she finished tying the lady up securely.

"Yeah, get out of here. I got it under control," Robyn said as she threw her head in the direction of the door.

Aries placed the duct tape over the lady's mouth and stood up. Aries headed out of the door and was on her way to the courthouse. She had to somehow get to the judge before the trial started at 10:00 A.M. She was determined to pull off this job, and her heart raced as she jumped into the car and headed toward the courthouse where the judge's chambers were located.

Aries' stilettos clicked against the courthouse's porcelain floors as she hurried down the corridor. Aries stopped by the directory and saw that Judge Cox's chambers were at the end of the hall. She looked down at her watch and saw that it was a half hour until the last day of trial began.

She proceeded down the hall, trying to figure out how she would pull this off. She had to leave her gun in the car, or else the metal detector would have picked it up. So, she would have to threaten the judge without a weapon and hope like hell he didn't call for the guards.

Aries approached the door and saw the judge with his back toward her as he put on his gown. He stood behind his desk and never even heard Aries slip in.

"Good morning, Judge Cox," Aries said as she bared a big smile.

"Sorry, my chambers are closed until after two," he said, expecting to see legal counsel from one of his upcoming cases. He never even bothered to turn around as he began to look in the mirror and fix his tie.

Aries quickly approached the desk and sat on the edge of it.

"Excuse me! I am not open until after two," he said as he turned around and saw the young lady becoming comfortable on the edge of his desk. His cheeks turned slightly blush red as he began to get angered at what seemed to be a lady with a big hearing problem.

"Oh, I am so sorry. But . . . I have to use your phone to make a quick call," Aries said, all while still smiling innocently. She picked up the phone and began to dial Robyn.

The judge became irate as he stormed to the phone and attempted to hang up the phone, but Aries' free hand gripped his, stopping him in his tracks. He was taken by surprise by the beautiful woman's quickness and strength and froze in amazement. He snatched his hand back and stood speechless.

"I think you want to hear this," Aries suggested as she pushed the speaker button and hung up the phone. "Put her on," Aries said calmly as she leaned into the speaker.

The judge was unsure of what was unfolding and had a confused look on his face. A brief moment of silence filled the air as the judge and Aries exchanged stares. What once was a beautiful smile on Aries' face turned into a menacing smirk.

The silence was broken by the sound of duct tape being ripped from skin and then followed by a scream.

"Honey! Help! They are in our house and . . ." a woman's voice shrieked over the speaker.

Aries could see the blood rush from the judge's face, making him look like he had seen a ghost. His skin turned pale, and he noticeably began to breathe heavily.

"Take her off!" Aries ordered. She then looked at the judge, who grabbed the left side of his chest. "Now, have a seat. It looks like you need one," Aries ordered, having total control of the situation. "Now listen and listen closely, because I'm only going to say this once.

Today you have to deliver a verdict. What I want—" Aries started to give the judge an ultimatum, but the sound of a gun blast erupted out of the speaker, making her flinch in surprise.

The judge yelled as he reached for the phone. His body jerked and he fell to his knees and immediately began to grab the left side of his chest while sweating profusely. He tried to yell for help, but nothing came out. He couldn't breathe, and he had shooting pains in his heart. He was experiencing a heart attack. The sound of the gunshot over the phone and the thought of his wife being shot sent him over the edge.

Aries' hands shook as she was taken by surprise by the gunshot. "Robyn!" she yelled as her eyes shifted back and forth out of nervousness. Aries listened closely and she heard the woman screaming.

"What the fuck happened?" Aries asked frantically as she couldn't figure out what was going on. In the meantime, the judge was dying on the floor. The plan that seemed to be perfect was crumbling right before their eyes.

Robyn kneeled on the floor with a smoking gun in her hands. The wife was crying hysterically, but Robyn had blocked out her cries. The only thing she could focus on was the eight-year-old girl who lay bleeding in the living room's entryway. Tears streamed down Robyn's face as her hands shook and her heart ached. Guilt overcame her as the eyes of the dead girl stared into nothing.

What Robyn and Aries didn't plan for was for the judge's daughter staying home sick and being there during the caper. Robyn accidentally shot the young girl when she came into the living room to ask her mom for more juice. Robyn's instinct was to shoot first and ask questions last. In her world, it was a good instinct to have, but in this case, it was the wrong move.

Robyn's phone was on the floor, and she could hear Aries screaming, asking what had gone wrong, but Robyn couldn't take her eyes off of the beautiful little girl who lay before her. She couldn't believe what she had just done and was speechless. At that very moment, Robyn had sold her soul to the devil, and there would be no coming back . . . and she knew it. The gunshot to the head solidified a front seat in hell for her.

She picked up her phone and pushed the end button. She then called 911 in tears.

"Hello, 911. What is your emergency?" the operator asked.

"I want to report . . ." Robyn's voice began to crack as the tears continued to flow. "I want to report a murder."

Aries hurried out of the courthouse, trying to be as discreet as possible and not draw any unwanted attention to herself. Her heart beat rapidly and her knees trembled as she dialed Robyn's cell and got no answer.

"Come on, bitch. Pick up de phone," Aries said as she pushed end and redial. Again, she got no answer as she reached the parking lot. She didn't know what was going on, and her mind was racing a million miles per second.

As she got into her car, she took a look around, making sure no guards were coming after her. She thought Robyn had shot the wife, but she could not understand why. "Damn, Robyn!" Aries yelled as she hit her steering wheel with both of her hands.

Aries sped off and merged into traffic heading back over to the judge's house. After that day, her life would never be the same.

Aries pulled onto the block of the quiet suburbs, and it looked more like South Central than the upscale area that it once was. Police cars and ambulances flooded the block. Neighbors stood at the end of their driveways trying to see what the spectacle was about.

Aries' heart dropped as she saw the police putting yellow tape on the door. She slowed the car to a snail's pace and closed her eyes. "Oh my God, Robyn. What happened?" she asked as she watched everything unfold.

She looked closer and saw Robyn being escorted by three police officers while handcuffed. It all seemed to happen in slow motion as she walked to the police car. Robyn noticed Aries' car at the end of the block, but quickly turned her head, not trying to draw attention to her crime partner.

A tear slid down Aries' face as she turned the car around and began to exit the block. She watched through the rearview as Robyn ducked her head into the back of the police car. Aries knew at that point, the Murder Mamas would be no more. She couldn't understand what happened inside of the house, and she had to find out on CNN.

Aries watched the television while at their hotel room and knew that she didn't have long before the police connected the dots and began to come for her. She looked at the two duffle bags on the bed and then the photo of her best friend on the television screen. It broke her heart.

The two duffle bags contained one million of Case's dollars, and she had no time to do anything else but run. She left the rented car in the parking lot and jumped into her own Cadillac STS with the money in the trunk. She had no idea where she was about to go, but she knew that it was imperative to get out of the city, for it would be on fire in due time. Tears streamed down her face as Bob Marley's "Redemption Song" lightly pumped out of the subwoofers.

Aries would run for five years, until her past came back to bite her.

Chapter Two

Aries' past flashed before her eyes in a matter of seconds, and when she came back to her present reality, she panicked. Afraid for her life, and more importantly the life of her son, she tried to slam the door, only for it to be stopped by Case's expensive Mauri gator shoe as he placed it in the threshold.

"Agh, agh, agh," he said as he put his hand on the door forcefully. "You not going to invite me in, Murder Mama?" he asked mockingly.

Aries hadn't thought she would ever see him again. She had put the distance of an entire ocean between them, and still he had found her. Her heart beat rapidly as the intensity from her fear instilled a helpless feeling in her gut. She knew the man in front of her well—too well—and was surprised that he hadn't shot her on sight.

"Please, my son is upstairs," she whispered, desperately hoping that he would show her more mercy than she had ever shown any of her victims.

"I have no interest in your son . . . and you have the power to keep it that way if you act right," he said seriously.

Aries stepped outside of her home and closed the front door so that she was standing on the porch. Her body was the only barrier between Case and her home. Silently she wished that she were strapped. She would not have hesitated to blow his brains out, but she was unarmed and more vulnerable than she had ever been in her life.

Before, she was a reckless soul who didn't care if she lived or died, but she was no longer the young hothead she used to be. Now she was accountable to others besides herself; responsible for the lives of others besides her own. She couldn't pop first and ask questions later.

"Are you here to kill me? If you are, I just ask that you not do it in front of my son, and leave my family out of this," she said as her chest rose and fell to an anxious, irregular beat.

Her eyes scanned the street as she searched for the goons who she knew Case had come with. A man of his stature kept protection around him. His hired guns were never far behind.

Case smirked as he noticed how perceptive Aries was. She had been out of the business for quite some time, but just like riding a bike, she would never forget how to do it. Her instincts were sharp, and he could see her mental wheels spinning.

Case decided to ease her mind and help her figure things out. "The roof across the street. The mail truck three houses down. The young man cutting your neighbor's grass next door," Case said.

"They're all yours?" Aries asked uncomfortably as she fidgeted nervously while attempting to eye all of her enemies at once.

Case nodded. "I don't leave home without 'em, love," he replied.

"All of that muscle for little old me?" she asked.

"I'm not a fool, Aries. You may have everyone else charmed with this Susie Homemaker role, but I remember what you used to be. My goon squad ain't afraid of the legend," he stated as he looked her up and

down, respecting her gangster and admiring her physique all at once.

"Give me a pistol and it'll make it a fair fight," she
shot back.

"I give you a pistol, you'll put two between my eyes,"
he replied with a charming smile as he stepped closer
to her, invading her intimate space.

"Why are you here?" she asked.

"The way I see it, you owe me a million dollars. I'm
here to collect," he stated bluntly. He nudged her to the
side with his shoulder and reached for the doorknob.
"Let's finish this conversation inside," he said with authority as he walked inside of her home, uninvited.

Aries scoffed at his arrogance and quickly followed
him inside, locking the door so that they would not be
interrupted. "I don't have the money, Case. It's gone,"
she said honestly. There was no way that she could
repay the debt. She and Robyn had split the money
and Aries had spent hers long ago. It had helped her to
build a new life.

"Well, that's neither here nor there, Aries," Case replied as he sat down on her leather couch and leaned
forward, his elbows resting on his knees as he looked
at her seriously. "You see, I paid you and your girl good
money to do a job that you botched." Case sneered as
he remembered how the island beauty before him had
gotten over on him. "I expect to be paid back," he said.

"I can give you a hundred thousand, maybe one-fifty.
My husband is an—"

Case cut Aries off and continued her sentence for
her. "Accountant. Prince Q. Coleman graduated from
Berkeley. Born to Gwenadette and Henry Coleman in
1979. Broke his right leg when he was ten years old.
Has one child, your son, and right now he is sitting at
a traffic light, bobbing his head to Bob Marley as he

makes his way to the office. A man riding a red Kawa-saki is conveniently sitting behind him, waiting for a phone call from me," Case stated, letting her know that he was well informed on her situation. Case had done his homework, and if Aries weren't so deathly afraid, she would have been impressed.

"You've said a lot, but still you haven't said shit. What do you want?" Aries asked, growing impatient. She knew that Case had an angle because he had waited too long to come after her. Although she had changed a lot of things about herself, her ability to read people had remained the same. This wasn't about the money.

"You owe me, Aries, and it's time that you paid up. I've got a job for you, and it would have paid a million dollars, but seeing as how I have a credit with you, you're going to do it without protesting."

"I'm out of the life. I don't do that anymore," Aries replied.

At that moment, her son came into the room, inter-rupting their conversation. Aries looked at Case ner-vously and went to pick up her son. She rubbed his face and head then brought him close to her chest, never taking her eyes off of Case.

"I can't do what you're asking me to do. I will pay you back the money . . . every dime. But I cannot go back to that life. I have a child to think about," she defended, her voice stern but her eyes pleading.

"Exactly," Case stated. "Think of him, Aries. It is in his best interest if you cooperate."

Aries heard the subtle threat and tears of pure rage filled her eyes. "Is that a threat?" she asked.

"It's a fact," he said. "Now, put your son in his room and let's discuss this business. Don't come back out here with no surprises, either . . . unless you want your husband to put you in the dirt before the week is out," Case replied.

Although he didn't feel threatened by Aries, he was well aware of what she was capable of. He respected her and had seen firsthand what she could do. He would never allow her pretty face to distract him. Sleeping on a woman like Aries could lead to his demise. What Leonardo did for art, Aries did for killing. She was a seasoned professional, and Case would never underestimate her. He placed his hand in his lap so that he had quick access to his pistol and waited patiently for her to reenter the room.

Aries rushed into the master bedroom and into her walk-in closet where the safe room was located. The room had never been used. She had never needed to rely on its security before, but for times like this, she was grateful that she had talked Prince into installing it in their home. She grabbed one of her child's toys off of her bed and hurriedly carried him into the room.

"You stay in here, baby. We are going to play a game. You stay in here and hide until Mommy comes back."

She placed him on the floor and exited the room, closing it and sealing him inside. Only she and Prince knew the code to open the door, so she was confident that her son would be safe in the event that things got ugly with Case.

She returned to the living room, and now that her greatest weakness had been concealed, her attitude had changed. Aries knew that her back was against the wall. She would have to comply with Case's proposition in order to clear the debt she had with him.

"What do you want me to do?" she asked as she sat down directly across from him.

She crossed her legs, and Case admired the contour of her smooth, thick legs. She was so exotic . . . so feminine. If he didn't know how she got down, he would have never believed it. He reminded himself to stay focused as he thought of the task he needed Aries to complete.

"I need you to murk a mayoral candidate," Case stated.

She shook her head in dismay, knowing that once she reopened this door, it wouldn't be as easy to close this time around. She had been lucky to get out of the game when she did; now he was thrusting her back into it against her will.

"What city?" Aries asked.

"Los Angeles," Case answered.

"What?" Aries gasped as her eyes widened in surprise. Aries wasn't a rookie and didn't have overzealous ideas of the things that she could pull off. She knew that this would have been hard to accomplish. She had thought he was going to put her onto something simple, but a political figure was an entirely different ball game. In the past she had relied on an entire crew. Her girls had been her eyes and ears. Things would not play out the same without her friends and the odds would not be in her favor.

"Do you know how hard it is to put a play down like that?" she asked. "It sounds like a suicide mission."

"For anyone else it would be," he complimented.

Aries absorbed the information and knew that she was about to get in over her head.

"I cannot do this. I worked in a team, Case. I can't pull this off. The job's too big," she protested.

"You're the only one who *can* do this," Case said. "I know how you get down, so stop playing with me, ma. Do what you do and put a toe tag on the nigga."

"And if I refuse?" Aries asked, feeling overwhelmed.

"Then you'll be a grieving widow sometime very soon," Case threatened without holding back. "It's not personal. It's business. You do this and your debt will be void. You already know the flip side," Case said calmly.

As much as Aries wanted to walk away from the proposition, she could not. A future that had been so clear to her the day before now held no direction. Case was mapping out the path that he wanted her to take, and to her dismay, it was a dangerous, slippery slope. If she wasn't careful, she could jeopardize her entire world. A deep sigh escaped her lips, signifying her submission to his request.

"What's his name?" she asked.

"Macy Sigel. He is a high favorite in the upcoming election. I don't want the nigga to make it to his inauguration," Case seethed, revealing his animosity toward the future mayor.

Aries' eyes closed into slits of suspicion as she watched his reaction to the mention of Macy Sigel. "Sounds personal," she commented.

"Nigga just forgot where he came from," Case shot back as he restored his facial expression to his normal collected visage. He caught himself revealing too much emotion and knew that he had slipped up. *A bitch like Aries will turn that shit on a nigga quick and use it to catch me slipping,* he thought.

"We came up together in Long Beach and went our separate ways after high school. I hit the block; he hit the books. He's bankrolled his entire career off of my street endorsements. I contributed heavily to his campaign, and he was supposed to turn a blind eye to the li'l paper I'm collecting from the streets. Now that he's gained some notoriety and he's in the forefront to win the election, his entire platform has changed. Now he's on some 'clean up the streets' shit, and it's interfering with my money. He has LAPD coming down hard and it's become a problem. That's where you come in. You're my problem solver."

Aries frowned, sensing that he was leaving something out of his story. She didn't believe that Case was revealing the entire story. Her intuition told her that he was leaving out vital pieces to the puzzle. "Look, Case. I need to know your history with this man. This isn't new to me, and I can hear it in your tone that this isn't just about the money. I have to know everything," she urged.

Case cleared his throat uncomfortably and leaned forward in his seat. He rubbed his goatee as he peered at Aries sharply. "He took something from me once before and I let it slide. I'm not taking no shorts this time around." Case sat back comfortably in the chair as he prepared to share the story of where the deceit and treachery first began. . . .

Case had stood outside of the club, shining like new money as he leaned on the hood of the all-red 1993 Beamer with BBS gold rims. His head rolled slowly to the right as he watched the fleet of ladies who walked past his car, begging to be seen in their skin-tight dresses and thick gold rope chains with matching bamboo earrings. He felt a hand turn his face away.

"Don't play yourself, Case. While you watching them, every other nigga in the spot is watching me," Fatima said arrogantly as she leaned in and kissed her man on the lips, leaving her cherry red gloss on his lips.

He put his hand on her behind and pulled her near, loving her flirtatious nature. She knew her status and wasn't intimidated by other chickens that chased after her man. "Let's just blow this spot. I've got a party for you back at my place," he whispered in her ear.

She slowly pushed him off as she ran a red-painted fingernail down the side of his face. "That party isn't going anywhere," she replied. "Besides, we can't leave. Macy is supposed to be meeting us here."

As soon as the words left her mouth, a white Saab pulled up beside them. Macy Sigel climbed out with his latest flavor of the month on his arm. Case and Macy greeted one another warmly as they slapped hands, embracing each other briefly.

"What up, baby?" Case greeted. "You looking good, family . . . Look at you. I see you shining with your jewels and your little ride. Somebody's getting money."

"Everybody's getting money," Macy replied as he smiled charmingly. He saw Fatima standing behind Case and moved him to the side to greet his girl.

"Hey, Macy," Fatima said as she kissed his cheek.

"Hey, baby girl," he replied as he kissed her cheek.

"Who's your friend?" she asked as she looked at the girl who was sitting in Macy's passenger seat.

"Nobody special, just a little entertainment for the night," Macy said conceitedly.

"You need to find some entertainment for life, fam, and quit messing with these skeezers," Fatima said playfully.

"Not everybody could be as lucky as my man here. They don't make 'em like you no more," Macy said as he turned and patted Case on the chest.

"I'm a lucky man," Case stated as he draped an arm around Fatima.

Macy's date emerged from the car, and the foursome entered the club, prepared to ball out for the night.

Popping bottles and grandstanding for the hood was all a part of the life of young Case and Macy. Coming up in Long Beach, California the pair had made quite a name for themselves. When the '80s ushered in the

crack era, Case and Macy quickly entered the game
and rose to the top. With their Mexico connection,
they supplied a large portion of L.A. with pure white,
while still running smaller trap spots on various blocks
as well. They wanted all the money and they didn't
discriminate against anyone. Whether it was a smoker
copping small amounts or a hustler copping ki's, they
served everyone and treated everyone the same. They
respected money and anyone who spent it with them.

As they partied and celebrated their success, they
watched as Fatima danced with a drink in her hand,
commanding the dance floor. The jewels that she
sported were compliments of Macy, and her hips hypnotized as she wound them to the slow beat. She noticed Case watching her and she gave him a sexy smile.

"This is the life, man. The beautiful women, the
money, the cars," Case said.

"It's temporary. If we stay in this for too long, we will
eventually fall off," Macy replied.

"You sure you want to give all of this up? We just
started seeing real paper, and you're ready to retire
already," Case commented while shaking his head. He
couldn't understand how he could give up a lifestyle
that was so lavish.

"I start school this fall," Macy replied. "I've stacked a
hundred thousand. That's enough to pay for four years
of tuition plus some."

"Here you go with that bullshit," Case answered. "If
you invest four years in the street, you'll have enough
to retire. Why would you waste your time at a fucking
college to end up making fifty thousand dollars a year?
We get that in a couple weeks, fam."

Macy knew that Case didn't understand. While it
was true that street money was fast money, it equaled
instability. At any moment his infamy could be taken

away from him. His education would be his forever and could elevate him to levels of power that he could never attain pushing coke. Macy saw the full picture and looked at the long-term perspective. The allure of the streets wasn't strong enough to trap him there. He had used it for what it was; now he was elevating.

"You don't get it, but in due time you will," Macy replied as he raised his glass to his mouth and downed the cognac in his glass.

Fatima came off of the dance floor laughing jovially, obviously lifted off of the liquor she had consumed. "Dance with me?" she said to Case as she pulled his hand.

"You know better," he said as he licked his lips and pulled her into his space.

The alcohol had her feeling extremely sexual, and she bit his earlobe gently as she whispered, "You're no fun."

Macy's date came over and pulled him onto the dance floor. "Come on, girl, he can handle both of us," she said as she snapped her fingers in the air.

Macy was reluctantly dragged onto the floor, where he was the envy of the crowd as he was sandwiched between two beautiful ladies. They did more actual dancing than he did; he just swayed back and forth in the same two-step as the women worked him over. Fatima worked him over, grinding in front of him but making sure to keep a respectable distance as his date danced behind him.

Case stood on the sidelines, cheering them on and laughing as he watched the love that his city showed them. A part of him felt a genuine sadness that his boy was leaving the game. They had always been a pair. Since the day they had made acquaintances in grade school, they had rocked with one another. Macy was the only nigga in the streets who Case truly trusted with his life. Things would be different once Case was left to tend to things alone. He would never tell Macy, but he would miss doing their dirt together. Case could do the math, however, and quitting the game wasn't something that added up in his mind. He was going to get it until the day that he couldn't get it anymore. Nothing could knock his hustle.

Macy is chasing the white man's dream. That degree shit ain't for us. He gon' get that shit and still be waiting on a white mu'fucka to give him something. I'ma make my own ends. I'm a boss, he thought arrogantly as he heard the DJ make the announcement for last call.

At that moment, one of their goons came up to him, appearing flustered and completely underdressed for the club.

"Case, we've been beeping you all night," the young man said nervously, appearing worried.

"My beeper's in the car. What's good?" Case asked, giving his worker his full attention.

"The spot over in Inglewood got robbed. They took us for thirty thousand dollars," the guy said, leaning close to Case's ear so that he could be heard over the music.

Case saw red as he thought about how he had just taken a loss. Case wouldn't have cared what the amount had been. Big or small, he wanted every dime of what he was owed. *I'm going to have to make a believer out of a nigga,* he thought angrily as he thought of how he was going to make an example out of whoever had tried to test him.

He walked over to Macy and calmly put his hand on his shoulder. "Somebody hit the spot. We've got to go," Case stated.

Macy's mood instantly transformed and his trigger finger began to itch as he followed Case out of the club. Although Fatima didn't know what was going on, she could tell from the look on Case's face that playtime was over. She was a hustler's wife and was well aware of the ups and down that came with being on the arms of men like Case and Macy. She followed their lead and walked out of the club without asking questions. Macy's lady didn't go so easily however.

"Why are we leaving? What's going on?" she asked annoyingly.

"It's better not to ask questions," Fatima whispered as she looped her arm inside of the girl's and they walked side by side behind their men.

Tension was thick as Case hit the top of his roof. "How the fuck anybody even know where that spot at?" he hissed.

"How much they take us for?" Macy asked, trying to remain rational, although his temper was flaring more and more by the second.

"Thirty," Case replied.

Macy paced back and forth as he grilled the young hustler who had delivered the news. With a lawyer's flair, Macy did everything to catch the kid up, but his story was consistent, and Macy finally concluded that he had nothing to do with the robbery.

"We've got to handle this tonight," Macy stated.

"I'll take care of it," Case stated.

"What?" Macy shouted.

"Take the girls home. I've got it," Case replied. He knew that his boy was ready to go legit, and he didn't want to complicate things by pulling him further and further in the game. The more you played, the harder it was to quit, and Case was trying to be supportive of Macy's decision.

Macy approached Case and stood face to face with him. "We're in this shit together, bro. What if you need my trigger?" he asked.

"I won't. I'm not going to put any major plays down without you. I'm just going to find out what the fuck is going on. Make sure the girls get in safe and wait for my call. I'll fill you in so that you don't miss a beat," Case stated. They slapped hands and Macy patted Case's back.

"You be careful, fam," Macy said.

Case nodded, kissed Fatima, and then hopped into his car, speeding out of the lot.

Macy ushered the ladies to his car and sped off, riding in silence as his anger boiled inside of him. He gritted his teeth and checked his pager anxiously to make sure that Case hadn't called him.

Fatima sat in the backseat, her mind spinning as tension ate away at the atmosphere inside the car. She knew that Macy would never speak about business in front of his new friend, but she desperately wanted to know what was going on. She had been around since before Macy or Case ever even knew what crack cocaine looked like, so she knew that he would put her up on game as soon as his girl was out of the car.

"I'm going to my mother's place out in Pasadena, so you might as well drop me off last," Fatima stated.

Macy looked at her curiously in the rearview mirror. He knew that her mother was deceased,m but didn't object as he dropped off his date first.

"I'll call you later," Macy said as he pulled up to her house.

Slightly vexed that she was being dropped off before Fatima, the girl smacked her lips and slammed the door as she got out of the car. Macy didn't even wait until the girl was safely inside before he pulled off.

"Nice girl," Fatima said sarcastically. She had been waiting all night to get on Macy for his choice in women.

He laughed slightly, knowing that Fatima was bourgeoisie. Case had created a monster when he had spoiled her. She was high maintenance and didn't like to fraternize with other women who weren't on her level. "You're a trip, ma," he replied.

"I'm just saying," she said as she smirked and shrugged her shoulders. "Now you gonna tell me what's going on or what?"

"Some niggas ran into one of the trap houses," Macy replied.

"Well, you know I'm going home with you. I'm not sitting by the phone at my place waiting for Case to call me. I want to be there when he contacts you. I have to know that he's all right," she said.

He could tell from the determined look on Fatima's face that it wasn't up for debate. He had known her long enough to know that he had no wins in an argument with her, so he gave in and headed to his place.

As Macy pulled up to his Hollywood condo, Fatima was impressed. Although Case was getting it, he had yet to let go of the hood, living in the heart of Long Beach. Macy, on the other hand, had stepped into the major leagues and was living well in the condo he was renting.

"I'm surprised you're even bringing me here," Fatima stated, knowing that no one even knew where Macy resided.

"What, you gonna rob me?" he asked, only half joking as he unlocked his door and welcomed her inside.

She stepped inside and was taken aback at how well his place was decorated. It was a far cry from the bachelor pad that Case lived in.

"Wow," she whispered.

"Don't let me find out you're materialistic," he stated, giving her a hard time.

She hit his shoulder with her clutch and then walked over to his leather sectional and took a seat.

"Can I get a drink or something?" she asked.

He pointed to the mini-bar in the kitchen and said, "Help yourself and use the phone in the kitchen to page Case. I'm going to go clean up a little bit."

Fatima paged Case and then fixed herself a drink as she waited patiently for the phone to ring. She nosily looked around for a woman's touch, but surprisingly found none.

She couldn't understand how a good catch like Macy was not spoken for. He and Case were the most sought-after young hustlers in Long Beach. While most were into the gang set, Case and Macy weren't into any color besides green. Every girl in the hood wanted a piece of them.

When Macy reentered the room, he was dressed in baggy gray sweat pants and a white V-neck T-shirt. Although he looked relaxed, she could see the stress in his frowned brow line.

"Is everything okay?" she asked.

"Yeah, I'm good, ma. I'm just feeling kind of fucked up. It's nights like this that make me feel guilty about leaving Case to hold things down by himself," he said.

"By himself? You're getting out?" she asked in shock.

He nodded his head and sat down across from her. "Entering school in the fall."

"School? Really?" she commented. She would have never suspected a hood nigga like Macy to have any ambition outside of the streets. "Interesting."

"You sound surprised," he replied.

"No, I just think that's good. Not a lot of brothers from Long Beach would be willing to give up all of this to put their head in a textbook," she said.

"You sound like your man. You think I'm stupid," Macy said.

"I think that it's attractive," Fatima replied honestly.

"The type of power I want transcends Long Beach. I know what it feels like to run a block. Now I want to know what it feels like to run boardrooms. I've conquered the streets. Now I'm trying to take on the world."

Fatima was impressed by Macy's intelligence, and she realized that there were many layers to the young hustler before her. Case had a one-track mind, but Macy was multi-faceted and he was showing her a side to him that made her look at him in a new light.

The phone finally rang, and Macy went to answer it. Knowing that very few people had the number, he expected it to be Case.

"Fuck took you so long to call me, fam? Your girl is over here worried sick about you," Macy stated.

"I thought you were gonna drop her home for me," Case stated.

"Wasn't no shaking loose from your broad, fam. You know how Tima is. Until she heard that you were safe, she wasn't budging out of my car," Macy replied.

Case chuckled slightly at his girlfriend's stubborn nature then replied, "Tell her everything's good. It's a thousand mu'fuckas over here with a thousand different stories. Don't worry about it though. You know we ain't taking no L's. We got eyes everywhere. Anybody spend a little bit of dough the next few weeks and we'll know who is behind it. Niggas is signing their own death certificates for sneaker money," Case said angrily.

"Don't make no moves tonight. Play it smart, Case," he replied.

"No doubt, baby. I'll fill you in more tomorrow," Case answered. "Tell Tima she can take her ass home now. As a matter of fact, take her to my crib and tell her I'll be home in the morning."

Macy hung up the phone and turned to an eager Fatima. "What did he say?" she asked.

"Everything's good. He's good. I'ma drop you at his place. He'll be there in the morning," Macy responded.

"The morning?" she shot back. "I don't want to be at his house in the middle of the hood by myself until morning! Can I stay here for a few hours? I hate being there without him. Somebody might try and steal me or something."

Macy couldn't help but laugh at her arrogance. "Girl, don't nobody want you," he stated as he poured a drink of his own. He brought the entire bottle over to his sitting area and then refilled Fatima's glass.

"Everybody want this in one way or another," she said as she sipped the alcohol and smiled sexily. "Bitches want to be me, and niggas want to be with me."

Macy couldn't argue with her because they both knew that what she was saying was true. She was queen bee around their way. From her beautiful exterior to her confident interior, she was envied by most.

"You're a pretty girl," Macy complimented, causing Fatima to smile. "But your arrogance is a turn-off."

"Excuse me?" she asked, her smile fading into an embarrassing frown.

"You're not humble. Humility is sexy. All that grand-standing you do is too flashy. Everybody already knows your name. You don't have to be so loud in order for people to see you and respect your position," Macy schooled.

Slightly embarrassed that Macy had called her out, she quickly looked away from him. No man had ever made her feel so insecure. She sat in front of him searching for something to say. Usually she prided herself on being confident, but Macy was the first person in her life to make her see how shallow she could be.

"I didn't know I came across like that," she whispered. "So tell me, Macy Sigel. What type of girl do you like? Since you claim I'm overconfident, you probably like them insecure and dependent on you, huh?" she asked. "When's the last time you even had a for-real girlfriend anyway? I've never seen you be serious about any girl. All of these chicks that be chasing after you and you haven't chosen one yet? What's the deal with that?" she asked nosily.

Macy sat back on his couch, throwing one hand on the back as he kicked his leg out in front of him. He sipped his drink. "You ask a lot of questions," Macy said playfully. "Come on, let me drop you off before it gets too late."

"You dodge a lot of questions," Fatima replied with a smile. "You can get on me, but when it's my turn, you're ready to wrap up the conversation and send me packing."

He chuckled softly. "It ain't like that, ma."

"Hmm, hmm," she said doubtfully. Suddenly she stood to her feet and walked past him as she headed toward the mini-bar.

"What you doing?" he asked.

"I'm looking foooorrr . . ." She searched the bar until she located the bottle of tequila. "This!" she finished as she turned toward him while holding up the bottle and two shot glasses with a devilish grin.

"What you gon' do with that? You don't know nothing about that," he answered.

"I tell you what, Macy. Let's play a game. I make a statement about you, and if it's true, you take a shot of tequila. If it's false, I take a shot," she proposed.

"I'm not into games," Macy shot back as he shook his head and enjoyed the mature cognac he was drinking. "Besides, I don't mix my alcohol. I'm already off this," he said, holding up his glass.

Completely ignoring him, Fatima carried the bottle back to the couch and sat directly next to him. She set up two shots and then sat back, tucking one foot beneath her bottom as she faced her body toward him.

"You like ghetto girls. That's why you brought little miss hot-ass mess to the club with you tonight," Fatima said. She held up one shot, and he nodded his head.

"You might as well kill that because that's false, baby girl," he answered.

She closed her eyes and poured the liquid down her throat. She cringed as she felt it warm her as it traveled down her throat. "Ooh," she whispered before bursting into laughter. "You want to ask a question, or you want me to keep going?" she asked.

He smiled at her, finding the game quite amusing. "Go ahead."

"Okay," she said, tapping her temple as if she were in deep thought. "You're not as cold-hearted as the streets think you are."

Macy had an intimidating reputation in the streets and because of his high body count at the young age of twenty, many people feared him. Fatima wasn't buying it though. She could tell from the look in his eyes that there was more to him; he just didn't share it with everyone. "In fact, I'ma go as far as to say that you don't love the game at all. It's just a means to an end for you."

Her line of questioning was much deeper than he had anticipated, and he looked her in the eyes for a long time before he finally reached for the shot glass and emptied it in his mouth. She had struck a nerve with him.

"Okay, my turn," he said. He poured two new shots and then continued. "If Case was a broke nigga, you wouldn't be with him."

His question caught her completely off guard, and her chin dropped to her chest. "So you think I'm a gold digger?" she asked, her feelings hurt. "After all these years I've known you . . ."

"I'm curious," he said. "You tell me what the answer is."

Fatima picked up the shot and then leaned over and squeezed the sides of Macy's face with one hand, opening his mouth. She slowly poured it inside, laughing as she watched some of it drip down the sides of his mouth. "Sorry to tell you, Macy, but you're wrong about me."

"I was wrong about that one statement. I have a hundred more," he replied.

The two went back and forth asking question after question, getting lit as they each consumed their fair share of alcohol. They were surprised at the revelations they uncovered about each other by playing such a trivial game, and they learned a lot about one another, sharing things with each other that they had never told anyone else.

Before they knew it, it was four o'clock in the morning and they were both toasted and laughing hysterically.

"I never knew you were so cool," Fatima admitted. "You're so serious most of the time. I like this part of you."

"I like this part of you, ma, the down-to-earth Tima. You're like my nigga right now," he answered.

She arched an eyebrow and said, "Oh, your nigga, huh?" She lifted the bottle of tequila that was mostly empty and then poured the last shot. "Okay, we have enough for one more round. Do you want to answer the question, or do you want me to?"

"Go ahead," he answered as his head fell back onto the couch, his body completely loose.

"I'll bet," she started as she closed the gap between them and climbed into his lap, "you have a big"—she planted a kiss on his neck—"long"—she wrapped her arms around his neck—"juicy dick," she finished as her lips found his and her tongue eased into his mouth. His dick instantly bricked and confirmed her statement.

"What are you doing, Tima?" he asked as he tried to pry her hands from around his neck. "You know this ain't right."

She reached down and put her hand inside his sweatpants and massaged his hard penis. "Ooh, but I wasn't lying, was I, Macy?" she asked. She retrieved the shot and fed him the tequila, moaning as she pressed her pussy against the bulge in his pants and began to hump him slowly.

"Oh shit, ma," he whispered. Her thick body felt so good pressed against his, but he knew that they were both intoxicated. This lusty encounter was nothing but the result of two attractive people having too much to drink.

"Stop, stop, ma," he whispered aloud, while silently cursing knowing that he wanted nothing more than to get things popping with his best friend's girl.

"Play the game, Macy. It's just a game. It's your turn," Fatima whispered as her tongue ran up and down his neck. She could feel Macy's dick growing and pulsating from her seduction. She was wet, and her pussy dripped in anticipation.

"Game's over, ma. We all out of liquor," Macy replied weakly, his tone husky and his eyes low from the effect of the liquor. He felt himself getting ready to cross the line. His dick was too hard and his head was too cloudy to talk himself off the edge.

Fatima stopped kissing him, stood to her feet, and then unzipped the side of her dress, stepping out of it. She stood in front of him wearing only her black panties and bra. "Then I guess we have to play for something else," she responded.

Macy sat back and watched as she unclasped her bra, freeing her D-cup breasts. Her brown nipples were large and erect, making his mouth water. Her breasts sat up so nicely that they bounced beautifully as she shimmied out of her tiny panties. He tried to think with his brain, but all of the blood in his body was rushing elsewhere. He had been with a lot of women, but Fatima by far was the most stunning chick he had ever seen. Her body was beautiful; even the minor stretch marks on the sides of her wide hips were flawless.

"It's your turn, Macy," she said.

He cleared his throat and stood, walking up on her and pinning her to the wall as he kissed her, their tongues performing a slow dance.

"You like to get this pussy licked. Your man don't do that right," he whispered as he picked her up and placed his hands beneath her backside while trapping her body between himself and the wall.

"Oooh, Macy," she moaned as they kissed feverishly.

He lowered his body until his knees were on the floor and her legs were wide open as she sat on his face. He licked her swollen clit, causing her body to tremble. She moved her hips in small circles, riding his face slowly.

"Oh my," she whispered. She couldn't even get the praises out of her mouth; it felt so good and she melted into him like butter as he raped her with his tongue.

They both knew that what they were doing was wrong, but they were too far gone to turn back, and the rapture that they were caught up in was too magnificent to deny. They would rather deal with the consequences than stop the bliss that they were experiencing at the moment.

He stopped right before she climaxed, and her breasts heaved as she begged him for more. "No, don't stop, Macy. Please," she whispered.

"I'm not stopping," he said as he scooped her up and carried her down the long hall that led to his master bedroom. He threw her onto the plush mattress and he stepped out of his pants, finally freeing his thickness and making her squirt.

She spread her legs and dipped her fingers inside her honey pot as she masturbated in front of him, closing her eyes and working herself over. He watched as he stood in front of her, stroking his shaft gently, tugging on his tool while preparing to enter her.

He reached to grab a condom that sat in clear view on his nightstand, but she grabbed his hand and pulled him on top of her.

"I want to feel you inside of me. We don't need that," she whispered.

"You trying to have my baby, ma," he responded jokingly.

"Yes, daddy. Put a baby in me, Macy," she answered, not caring if he planted a millions seeds in her, as long as he stroked her right.

At that moment, Case was the furthest thought from either of their minds, and when Macy entered her for the first time, he promised himself that no other man would ever enter her again, including Case. Her pussy was like heaven, and he wanted to be her only god.

She brought her hips up to match him stroke for stroke as he dug deep into her, knocking on her G-spot. Their bodies merged so well that it felt like they were meant for one another. Fatima didn't know if it was the fact that she was sexing a man that was forbidden to her or if Macy was just that good, but it was undoubtedly the best dick that she had ever had.

"This my pussy?" Macy asked her while putting his thing down. He was hitting her so good that her fingernails dug into his back, leaving her mark.

"Yes, Macy, it's yours," she moaned.

"You gonna give my shit away?" he whispered.

"No, baby. Ooh, it's yours. I swear I'm never giving it away," she promised. "I love you, Macy."

They both stopped and stared at each other; Macy still filled her as her legs trapped him inside. They both breathed heavily and she rubbed the side of his face gently with her hand as she looked him in the eyes.

"What?" he asked, thinking he had heard her wrong.

"I don't want to be anybody's girl but yours, Macy. I love everything about you."

Macy stole the words from her tongue as he kissed her deeply and took her to ecstasy as he continued to sex her until indeed his seed spilled into her.

He never said he loved her back that night, but in the months to come, they grew closer with each passing day. Their secret affair alienated Case, until eventually he was no longer a part of the picture.

It was a summer of change for all of them—one that they would never forget.

Chapter Three

"So you want him dead because of a woman," Aries concluded once he had finished his story.

"No, I want him dead because of the blatant disrespect," Case corrected. "By the end of that summer she was his girl. I caught her at his dorm room, sleeping naked in his bed one day while he was at class. They weren't expecting me. I just popped up. That was the first time he decided to touch what belonged to me. I let my issues with him go once before because I knew that she deserved a nigga like Macy. I took the higher road; this time I want what's mine."

Aries nodded her head. She had gotten rid of people for much less. Money and women were usually the motivation for murder, and Macy was about to fall victim because of his trespasses. He had alienated the one man who had helped him reach legitimate success, and Aries was the Grim Reaper. It pained her to agree to the terms. Her road to redemption had been interrupted, and she would have to leave her family for a while to get the job done.

"I know that this may be too much to ask, but I'll need some financial stability to do this for you. I need a place—a nice place," she added. "A presidential suite at the Ritz would be nice. I'll also need guns and a car . . . on you."

He nodded. "Done."

"Now get out of my house," she spat as she stood to her feet while glaring at Case in contempt.

"I'll be in touch," Case said as he gave her a dazzling white smile and stood to his feet. He followed her to the door, watching her behind sway as it hypnotized him. He shook his head because it was a shame that Aries was who she was. If she were any other woman, Case would have definitely come at her. She would probably be wifey, but the path she had chosen made her spoiled goods.

No hustler could ever trust a Murder Mama. They were too ruthless, and Aries didn't exclude anyone from her wrath. Anybody could get it. *Including you,* she thought silently as she watched Case walk out of her home and pull away from the curb.

Aries stood in front of the mirror breathing heavily as she gripped the sides of the sink's vanity. Stress plagued her as she thought of Case's proposal. He was forcing her hand, making her go back to a lifestyle that she no longer believed in. Her mind spun as she thought of how to get herself out of the situation, but deep inside she knew that the only way out was compliance. She had to do what he wanted her to do.

She kicked herself for coming out of hiding and showing her face in California. Going to Robyn's execution had put her at risk; it had put her family at risk. It had been stupid. She was positive that it was how he had located her.

She thought of killing Case. *I should body that nigga for even coming to my doorstep,* she thought angrily as her head hung in indecision. Aries was seriously contemplating that option, but the reality was that Case was too powerful to touch. He had a crazy goon squad with numbers into the hundreds, and she was only one woman. She couldn't take on the world, and it hurt her pride to give in to his demands.

Back in the day, no one would have ever been able to come at her that way. She popped niggas like kernels and didn't think twice about whose boyfriend, son, or father she was putting to rest. Case, however, wasn't just any old mark. He was a boss—a boss who moved smart and who had enough resources to locate her after half a decade.

A hand on the back of her neck caused her to flinch. She turned around swiftly and grabbed the hand tightly, prepared for a fight.

"Rachel, it's just me," Prince said.

She exhaled as she walked into his chest and rested her head against it. "Oh my God. You scared me," she whispered.

Just that quickly, an inclination to take a life had come back to her, but when she realized it was only her husband, she calmed down. She knew the emptiness that came along with committing that type of crime. It had taken her so long to fill her soul and truly live again. Once she went back to her old ways, she wasn't sure if she would make it out. Rachel Coleman would die in the world that Aries used to dwell in.

"You're trembling. What's wrong?" Prince asked.

"I just had a bad dream. I can't sleep," she lied as she squeezed him tightly. "Just hold me."

His warm embrace did nothing to ease her heart, and as they made their way back into their bedroom, her senses were on full alert. Every little noise made the hairs on the back of her neck stand tall. "I'm going to get Tre," she said. "I want him in here with us tonight."

Prince lay back in their bed and mumbled an okay as Aries left the room. She peeked in on their son and then bypassed his room momentarily so that she could check the rest of the house.

It was pitch black in the Caribbean home, and she turned on no lights. She knew her house better than anyone else, so if someone was inside of it, the darkness would work to her advantage. She no longer owned a gun, and made a mental note to purchase one as soon as possible.

Aries crept to the kitchen and reached into her knife block, running her hands over the many knives until she located the large chef's knife. She paused in silence as she listened to the sounds of her house. She heard many sounds. The creak of the air conditioning as it turned on, the sound of the wind causing her white picket fence to open and close on its own: These were all sounds that were familiar to her. She was trying to decipher anything that sounded out of place.

When she was sure that nothing was moving inside, she turned on the lights. She went from room to room with the knife ready, but found nothing. She sighed in relief. *I'm tripping,* she thought. *No one is here.*

She retreated to the second floor and grabbed her son out of his bed. She took him into her bedroom, where Prince was snoring loudly. He slept so comfortably, completely oblivious to the sudden threat that had entered their lives.

She tucked the knife beneath her mattress and lay down with her son in her arms. She kept him near as her eyes scanned the room. She couldn't relax, not when she knew that her enemies were so close.

She had to make this problem disappear, and she knew that it meant returning to L.A. to repay a debt to her old friend Case.

Chapter Four

Aries watched Prince dress for work and dreaded what she was about to do. She was tired of lying just to survive. No matter how hard she tried to live her life the right way, wrong had a way of finding her. In order to keep up one lie, she had to tell another lie, and another and another. It was all too much to remember, but at this point there was no turning things around. Aries was so far removed from the truth that not even she knew what it was anymore.

Aries smiled as she watched the love of her life struggle with his tie, and she stood up to help him. Her short silk robe hugged her wide hips as she walked over and reached up to adjust it for him.

"What would I do without you?" he asked playfully as he stood tall while she dressed him. She tied his tie and then grabbed his jacket, holding it out for him so that he could slip his arms inside.

"You'll never have to think about that," she replied, hoping that it was true.

"I think I need to go back to the States for a while, Prince," she said, throwing out the bait.

"For what? You just came back, Rachel. We may as well move back there you're back and forth so much," he stated with displeasure.

"It's my mother. She's not getting any better, and she needs me. It won't be too long. The doctor says she won't live long, and I just want to be there with her.

No one should have to die alone, Prince. Besides, I'm her daughter. I just need to go be with her," Aries said, pleading her case so convincingly that her eyes pooled with emotion. Little did Prince know Aries had been a motherless child since she was a young girl.

Prince sighed as he felt sympathy for his wife. "How long will you be gone?" he asked.

"I'm not sure. As long as it takes," she responded. "Hopefully she will go peacefully and in a few weeks I'll be back home. I wish that I could take you with me, but you have work and I don't want Tre to see her like that."

"It's not like she'll want to see either of us anyway. She never approved of our marriage from the beginning," Prince stated. "Now you want to go away to her aid without telling me when you will be back. That's a lot to ask for a woman I've never met."

Aries had told Prince that she and her mother had never seen eye to eye. He was under the impression that her mother disapproved of their relationship. "What type of mother is she? She doesn't even want to meet your husband and child," he snapped.

"She's the only mother I've got," Aries defended. She sighed and wrapped her arms around Prince's neck and then kissed his neck sensually. "Please, baby. I promise you that after this trip I will be all yours. You and Tre will be my only priority after I handle this last thing."

Prince couldn't resist his woman and easily gave in. "Okay. We'll be here waiting for you. Just make sure you don't let another man have any of what's mine," he said as he put his finger in her mouth and then toyed between her thighs.

She was wet and more than willing to please him, but he was running late. He sighed, knowing that he couldn't stop to put his woman to bed. He had a very important meeting to get to and pulled away from her. "I'ma handle that when I get home. When do you need to leave?" he asked her.

"As soon as possible. I'll probably book the first flight leaving out tomorrow morning," she answered.

Prince shook his head, not really wanting to see her go, and said, "Handle everything that you need to handle, Rachel. I want you home with me and our son. No more trips overseas after this. After you bury your mother, bury all of the baggage that keeps pulling you back there."

"Okay," she answered. Aries had no intention of leaving things undone this time around. She was going back for the last time. She was going to make sure of it.

Chapter Five

Macy Sigel waved at the crowd of people as he stepped off of the stage. His tailored suit and diamond cufflinks added to his natural charm and attractive appearance. The people loved him, and he had the hearts of the entire city. Little did they know that he was once one of the most successful drug lords that Los Angeles had ever seen. The event was held in the convention center and the place was jam-packed. He had just delivered a speech and received a standing ovation from the community's patrons. The rally was held to stop the violence and growing drug problem in the city. Macy's bodyguards waited for him at the bottom of the steps, all of them draped in all black with black shades.

"The car is waiting for you in the back, sir," one of the bodyguards said as they made their way through the crowd and toward the back exit.

Macy waved as he disappeared into the back. As soon as he got out of view of the public, his smile turned into a serious glare, and one of his bodyguards handed him one of his Cuban cigars, his favorite. Macy lit it up and took a drag. He loosened his tie and dipped into the limo that was waiting near the back door.

He was accompanied by five bodyguards; all of them were strapped liked the al-Qaeda and ready to pop off at any suspicious person who ran up. Macy's past life made him a moving target, and he knew that security was a must. At one point, Macy was deep in the drug game, and a lot of people felt that he owed them something. Macy understood that and took extreme precaution in protecting himself and his family.

He looked down at his Rolex and noticed that it was nearing six o' clock. It was his fifteen-year anniversary, and he had a special dinner planned for his wife and himself. He instructed the driver to head to the private venue where the party was being held, and just like that, they were on their way.

Fatima Sigel smiled as she watched her husband and his entourage enter the ballroom. Macy's close friends and some of his business associates filled the room along with Fatima's friends and family. They were all there to celebrate their anniversary, and the place was extravagant, to say the least. Champagne- and gold-colored décor laced the venue, and the sound of smooth R&B pumped out of the speakers. Expensive champagne flowed into fluted glasses as the waiters kept no hand empty. It was a great mood for what was to be a joyous celebration.

Macy and Fatima locked eyes as Macy made his way over to her table. Along the way, Macy was stopped by various people giving him handshakes and small talk, but he quickly made his way to his beautiful wife.

"Happy anniversary, sweetheart," Macy said in his low baritone as he bent over and kissed Fatima on her forehead.

"Hey, baby," she said as she smiled and watched him as he took a seat next to her.

"I didn't see Boomer. Where is he?" Macy said, referring to their eighteen-year-old son.

"I don't know," Fatima answered as she looked down at her watch. "He definitely should be here by now. He promised me that he would come. I don't know about that boy sometimes," Fatima said as she shook her head and was noticeably disappointed.

"Look, don't worry about that. Let's dance," Macy suggested as he tried to take her mind off of their son not showing up to the event. He smiled and stood up as he extended his hand for her.

"Sure. I would love to," Fatima accepted as she grabbed his hand and headed for the dance floor.

Macy held his wife close, and he could smell her sweet perfume as he pulled her close. He looked at her with his piercing eyes and released a warm smile.

"How was the rally?" Fatima asked as she wrapped her arms around Macy's neck and slowly two-stepped to the sounds of R. Kelly.

"It was okay. The house was packed," Macy said as he shrugged his shoulders. He opened his mouth to say something else, but the sounds of the door being opened got his attention.

In walked Boomer with his best friend, Fruit. They were obviously out of place, and the overbearing smell of marijuana followed them. It was a black tie affair, but Boomer had taken it upon himself to wear baggy street clothes and gaudy jewelry. He and his friend came in laughing loudly, and they stuck out like two sore thumbs as all eyes seemed to drift to them.

Macy instantly shook his head as he knew that Boomer was about to embarrass him in front of all of his colleagues. Macy clenched his jaws tightly as he watched Boomer make his way toward them, slightly staggering.

"Oh God," Fatima whispered as she looked in her son's eyes, noticing that they were bloodshot red. She dropped her head in shame seeing her only son that way. The tips of Boomer's nostrils were also red, signaling that he was high off more than weed.

Quiet mumbles and whispers began to fill the room as the guests chatted about the hoodlum who had just entered the party. Macy acted quickly and headed toward Boomer, trying to stop him before he reached his mother. This was her day, and Macy wasn't going to let anyone bring her down on their anniversary.

The closer Macy got to Boomer, the stronger the weed aroma grew. Macy looked into Boomer's eyes and knew that he was high as a kite. He had been around long enough to know that Boomer was flying off of more than just a little weed, however.

"Let's go. Don't let your mother see you like this," Macy said as he threw his arm around Boomer and smiled, trying to not make a scene. He turned Boomer toward the door and began to walk him out, but Boomer had other plans.

"Get yo' hands off of me!" Boomer yelled as he snatched away from Macy.

Macy quickly fixed his tie and checked his cufflinks as he smoothly played it off, still having a smile on his face. Boomer's friend Fruit, a skinny kid, stepped to the side and found everything to be funny. He smiled as the drama unfolded before his eyes.

"Do not do this to your mother, Boom. Today is a special day for her," Macy said in almost a whisper. However, the sternness was still evident in his voice.

"What the fuck you mean? What? You embarrassed?" Boomer asked as he threw his arms up, causing a scene. "You don't want everyone to know that your son is a street nigga?" Boomer said as he got louder with each word.

At that point, the DJ had cut the music and everybody's attention was on the spectacle that was about to unfold. The two men locked eyes, and it was undeniable tension between the two of them.

"This is neither the place nor time for your bullshit," Macy said, keeping his voice low, but never breaking the piercing stare he had on the young man who stood in front of him.

"Well, when is the right time, huh? Don't want everybody to know that your family isn't perfect, huh?" Boomer said as he saw Macy's bodyguards begin to make their way toward him.

"I see this isn't going anywhere," Macy said as he turned his back and pulled out the cigar that was in his top pocket. He placed it in his mouth and shook his head in disgust. Boomer and he had reached a boiling point, and the mutual dislike for one another finally came to the surface.

Macy always resented Boomer because he knew that he wasn't his biological child. Fatima never admitted that Boomer wasn't his, but Macy knew the truth. Maybe it was the light-skinned complexion of Boomer, or maybe even the lack of ambition that Boomer had, which was totally opposite of Macy's sharklike demeanor. They never spoke on it, and Macy never questioned his wife openly out of respect. Nevertheless, deep in Macy's heart, he knew the truth about the situation. He never pressed the issue, not wanting to dig deep into something that would eventually cause his family heartache.

Boomer also had a deep hatred for Macy. He expected things to be handed to him, and Macy wasn't having it. Macy never gave Boomer anything for free. Macy was only trying to prepare Boomer for the real world, but Boomer took it as Macy not loving him. Boomer was what you call a wannabe. He wanted to be the next street kingpin. He desired to live the fast life, and he wanted that title "kingpin" to be handed to him.

He had heard about how Macy was big in the streets, and he wanted to be what Macy once was. Macy never took Boomer down that road, for fear of the potential outcome. He already knew that Boomer wasn't built for the drug game. To be honest, Macy thought Boomer was too foolish to move drugs, so he never introduced it to him. And for that reason, Boomer hated his so-called father.

"Fuck you, Macy Sigel. You ain't nobody's mayor. You a goon just like me! All of those fancy suits and bodyguards can't hide who you really are, playboy," Boomer yelled as he breathed heavily and twisted his face up.

Boomer's friend stood next to Boomer and watched, not believing that Boomer was going off like he was. Fruit already heard stories about how ruthless Macy was in the past, and honestly, Fruit began to get nervous.

Macy didn't even give him the respect to turn around and look at him. He just lightly chuckled and shook his head as he lifted a lighter to spark flame to his cigar. Boomer continued his rant.

"To tell you the truth, you's a bitch!" Boomer yelled, enunciating every word.

"Boomer!" Fatima yelled as she stood up, having seen enough. Just as Fatima was screaming her son's name, Boomer, high as a kite, threw a punch, trying to connect with the back of Macy's head.

Macy, without even seeing it coming, stepped to the side. Boomer's swing missed and sent him crashing onto the ground. Macy smoothly slid his free hand into his pocket and looked over at his approaching bodyguards.

"Escort these gentlemen out and make sure he gets home safely," Macy said as he stepped over Boomer and walked over to Fatima, who had tears in her eyes.

The guards grabbed Boomer and Fruit and quickly guided them out. Macy looked at the DJ and nodded, signaling him to start up the music, and on cue, the sounds of smooth jazz pumped out of the subwoofers. Macy quickly wiped away Fatima's tear before it reached her cheekbone.

"Come on, let's dance, baby," Macy asked as he smiled from ear to ear.

"I tried to raise him the best way I knew how, but he—" Fatima said before Macy gently placed his finger on her lip, hushing her.

"Don't worry about it, baby. He is just high out of his mind. He just has to sleep it off," he whispered, trying to smooth over the tense situation. Macy didn't express it, but he knew that Boomer was going to be a problem—a real bad problem.

Boomer drove down the highway doing almost one hundred miles per hour. His eyes were bloodshot red and his temper was past his boiling point. He gripped the steering wheel tightly as he thought about how much he hated Macy.

"I can't stand that nigga," Boomer said through his clenched teeth. He quickly dipped his head and used his nose as a vacuum, sucking up the cocaine that sat on the book in his lap. He slightly swerved, causing Fruit to get uneasy.

"Whoa! Nigga, keep your eyes on the road," Fruit said as he gripped the door handles and braced himself.

"Relax, scary-ass nigga. I got this," Boomer said as he wiped his nose and felt the rush of the grade-A cocaine working. Boomer kept thinking about the smug look on Macy's face, and it only enraged him more.

"That nigga thinks he's untouchable. I will show him, though. Trust that!" Boomer said as he tried to think of a way to get Macy back.

Boomer and Fruit had been smoking weed and sniffing cocaine most of the day, and he had never been as high as he was at that moment. He was past high; he was on another level.

"What you going to do?" Fruit asked, halfway instigating the situation.

"I don't know, but I'm going to do something. That nigga think he better than me. You know he never let me call him Daddy. He always told me to address him as Macy. Do you know what that does to a little boy's mind? Every kid around me got to call their father Dad, but no, not me. I hate him!" Boomer said, getting more upset with each word that left his mouth.

"I can't believe you talked to Macy Sigel like that. I heard stories about that nigga. He is a hood legend. I heard that Macy shot off a nigga's finger for stealing ten dollars from him. Ten measly-ass dollars!" Fruit said, only pouring fuel on Boomer's fire.

Boomer knew that Fruit was telling the truth because Boomer was in the car when Macy rolled up on the guy who had shorted him. Macy thought Boomer was asleep, but he was playing possum and saw the whole thing. He was only nine years old at the time.

"Macy ain't shit. He ain't a real street nigga. But me, I'm a street nigga to the core. I'ma show his ass a li'l something. He want to disrespect me in front of all of those people; I'll show him," Boomer stated as a thousand and one ideas bombarded his thoughts.

He began to think sinisterly, and he quickly began to think about the stash that Macy had hidden in a safe behind a painting on the wall. Macy used to stash his street money there back in the day, but after he began to get into politics, he let it sit. Boomer had recently begun to chip off of the stash, knowing Macy wouldn't find out. But now Boomer had a better idea. He wanted to take the whole stash. It was over a million dollars in the oversized duffle bag—all dirty money.

"Want to get some money?" Boomer asked, hoping his right-hand man was down for what he had in store.

Aries sat back in her car and watched through binoculars as two guys came out of Macy's residence with two large duffle bags. She had been camped a few houses down from Macy's gated residence, trying to think of a plan to get him.

Who are these niggas? Aries thought to herself as she saw the men stuff the duffle bags in the back of a silver Benz and then get into the car. She looked closely as she camped out, trying to find the best angle to get to Macy.

Macy and Fatima came in the house, both in laughter as they enjoyed a good joke. They had a wonderful dinner and enjoyed a long stroll along the beach as they reminisced about old times. Macy immediately went to the security pad that was on the wall and pushed in a code, disabling the alarm. He then flicked the light switch on and then off, signaling his bodyguard that they were in safe. Macy looked out of his window and saw his driver and head bodyguard pull off.

"I had a wonderful time, Macy Sigel," Fatima said as she crept up and hugged him from behind. She smiled, closed her eyes, and rested her head on his back. Macy turned around and looked in Fatima's eyes.

"You are the love of my life. I am happy to have celebrated fifteen years with you as my beautiful bride," Macy said in his deep baritone. He leaned down and began to passionately kiss his wife.

They both felt the electricity in the air and the sexual tension had been building up all day. Macy slowly reached his hand behind Fatima and unzipped her dress. Fatima's favorite black dress fell to ground, and Macy stepped back to enjoy the view. She was still as beautiful as the first day he had met her. She wore no panties and had on a lace Victoria's Secret bra. The expensive bra held up her perky silicone breasts that Macy had purchased for her birthday a couple years back. The sight was eye candy to Macy, and he was ready to lick the sweet specimen that stood before him.

Fatima did a little pose, showing off her great body, and released her fake tits from her bra. Her erect nipples pointed straight forward as she squeezed and jiggled them. She turned around and headed to the bedroom, purposely switching hard so her man could get a peepshow.

Macy grabbed his pole that began to rise in his slacks as he licked his lips, putting LL Cool J to shame. The sound of his wife's stilettos clicking against the marble floor drove him even crazier as he imagined himself lying beneath her as she rode him slowly. Fatima grabbed a bottle of wine off of the wine rack and disappeared into the room.

Macy dropped his pants and quickly followed his wife into the back. As Macy headed to the master bedroom where Fatima was waiting, he saw the Martin Luther King painting on his wall. He noticed that it was slightly crooked, leaning to the left. He stopped in his tracks and frowned up, sensing that something was wrong. He quickly lifted the painting on the wall and looked at the secret safe that he had built into the wall. Macy's heart dropped when he noticed that the safe was slightly cracked and not closed like he had left it.

"Fuck!" Macy yelled as he snatched open the safe and saw that it had been cleaned out. A small piece of paper sat in the safe, and Macy angrily snatched it out. It read: FUCK YOU. Macy clenched his jaw so tightly it seemed as if he would crack his teeth.

Fatima came running into the hallway in concern. "Baby! Baby, what is it?" she asked as she looked on in confusion.

Macy held up the note and shook his head from side to side. "Boomer. It was Boomer," he said as rage built up in his heart. Macy, out of pure anger, punched a hole through the wall. It wasn't the fact that he lost the money; it was the fact that it had been taken from him by his own son. Macy's street instinct began to kick in, and all he saw was red. Disloyalty was unacceptable in Macy's book, and Boomer had crossed the line.

Chapter Six

Sweat dripped off of Boomer's brow as he pumped feverishly, pounding the small white girl who bent over in front of him. He leaned over and sniffed the coke that was put on her back by Fruit. The small-framed blond hooker threw her ass back, smacking it against Boomer's pelvis. Fruit sat at the table across the room watching as he periodically used a card to shove cocaine into his nostrils. He watched closely as his partner aggressively sexed the cheap whore.

"Yes! Yes!" she yelled as she bent over the bed while getting thrashed.

Boomer had cocaine residue on the tip of his nostrils and the drug had him horny as ever. The smell of sex was in the air, and the lavish hotel room had coke everywhere. Boomer had purchased nine ounces of pure coke and a hooker, all at the expense of Macy's drug money.

Boomer let out a loud grunt and began to shake vigorously as he was experiencing his fifth orgasm in a matter of an hour. He was on a total rampage, and the more coke he did, the bigger rush he got. Never once did he think about the consequences of his actions. He robbed one of the most ruthless men the West Coast had ever seen. Although Macy had left the street life and gotten into politics, his gangster was still buried deep inside of him.

Boomer pushed the girl out of the way and walked over to the table completely naked. He dipped his whole face into the coke pile and sniffed deeply. He quickly jerked his head up and held it back to prevent his nose from running.

"You need to ease up on that shit," Fruit suggested, noticing that Boomer had sniffed three times more than him. They had been in the hotel room for three days straight getting high, and Fruit was beginning to come to his senses.

"Nigga, I got this! I am just getting started," Boomer said as a crazed look formed in his eyes. "I wish I could see that nigga's face when he went home to an empty safe," Boomer said as he smiled from ear to ear.

Fruit shook his head in resentment as he thought about what they had just done. "He's not going to know we did it, is he?" Fruit asked, trying to make sure that he didn't get any backlash from the caper.

Boomer didn't answer. He just focused his attention on the hooker, who was left lying on the bed, breathing heavily.

"You want some of that?" Boomer asked Fruit as he pointed at the stripper's pink middle.

"Nah, go 'head," Fruit said as he avoided looking in the direction of Boomer, who was completely naked and sweaty. Under normal circumstances, he would not have turned down a piece of ass, but he was too nervous to even get erect.

Boomer then grabbed a card off the table and scooped some of the coke off of the pile. He sprinkled a line on his erect pipe and carefully walked over to the bed and stood over the hooker. She rose up and sniffed the blow off of his rod. She fell back on the bed and let the drug run its course. Boomer wasted no time. He got on top of the girl and began to sex her once again.

***

Macy was in deep thought as he paced his office back and forth and rubbed his goatee. "I can't believe that li'l nigga crossed me like that," Macy said to his head bodyguard, who went by the name of Edris, aka, Big E.

"How do you know it was him? Are you for sure?" Edris asked as he stood by the door with his hands crossed in front of him.

"I'm telling you, it was him. He was the only one who knew where the safe was. The combination was his mother's birthday and he knew that. You saw the shit he pulled at the anniversary dinner," Macy said, refreshing Edris' memory.

"Yeah, the li'l nigga was bugging out. What do you want to do?" Edris asked, as he was prepared to do whatever for his boss.

"The way I'm feeling right now . . ." Macy said as he walked over to his cabinet and pulled out the expensive bottle of Scotch and poured himself a shot. He tossed the shot back and continued his sentence. "I could whack his ass." An uncomfortable silence filled the air as Macy's temperature began to rise. He felt more disrespected than he ever had. He honestly believed that Boomer wouldn't hesitate to kill him if the opportunity presented itself. Boomer had been disrespecting him ever since he got the position as mayor, and it got worse with time. Macy had to make a big decision.

"We have to find him before he blows all of that money," Macy said as he slammed the shot glass on the desk.

A knock on the office door sounded just as the glass hit the table, and both of their eyes shot to the door. Macy looked down at his watch and noticed that it was just a tad past five o'clock. The receptionist shouldn't have let anybody in after business hours.

E clicked his gun off of safety that rested in his holster and opened the door. He saw that it was a cleaning lady and immediately covered his weapon and let her in.

"Oh! I am so sorry. I thought you guys had left. I'm with the cleaning service," the lady said. She held a bucket and broom in her hand.

"Don't worry about it, sweetheart. We were just on our way out," Macy said as he grabbed his suit jacket and put it on. He and E headed toward the door, and Macy began to put the plan together in his head on how he would handle Boomer. Macy waited until they got in the hall to speak on it.

"Put the word out on the street. Ten stacks to whoever can tell me where he is. I don't want anybody to touch him. I just want him brought to me before he blows through my fucking paper. I need to find that nigga before he does something stupid. His mother is at home going crazy, and I need to settle this bullshit," Macy stated as they headed out of the back entrance and into his tinted truck.

"I am on it, boss," Edris said as he opened the door for Macy and then headed to the driver's side to chauffeur. Macy still had pull in the streets, so it wouldn't be long before Boomer was caught.

Aries threw the broom and bucket down in frustration as she snatched off the wig that she wore. She was so close to Macy but couldn't do anything because of the bulky security guard that was present. She had finally gotten close to Macy and she couldn't do a thing.

"Fuck!" she said under her breath as she realized that she would have to be more strategic when dealing with Macy. He never was alone, and that made her job a difficult task. Aries headed out of the office.

She would have to go back to the drawing board. She had to find a way to finish the job—for her family's sake.

Boomer watched as the blond hooker danced for him completely naked. She stumbled as she tried to balance herself on the six-inch heels. Her hair was wild and her nose was bright red, and her white skin seemed to be burned because of the blow she had sniffed. Her red stilettos tantalized Boomer as he licked his lips while in complete ecstasy.

"Daddy, give me another hundred," she begged as she sloppily played with her vagina.

Boomer, without hesitation, reached into the bag and pulled out a stack of money. He threw it in the air, making it rain fifty and one hundred dollar bills.

Fruit sat in the corner smoking weed and observing his friend being careless. "Yo, you bugging right now," Fruit yelled from across the room as he witnessed his partner become frivolous with the dirty money.

"Nigga, mind your own business. I got money to blow," Boomer said as he sat back in his chair like a fat cat without a care in the world. The hooker went into her purse and pulled out a pipe.

"Do you mind?" she asked as she held the pipe up in the air.

Fruit's eyes instantly got big as he realized that the girl was about to smoke crack.

"Do your thing," Boomer said as he began to stroke his dick and lick his lips.

The girl then cocked her head back and placed the rock in the tip of the pipe. She closed her eyes and lit up the crack cocaine. The sound of crackling filled the air, followed closely by a burning aroma. She walked over to Boomer and put the pipe in Boomer's mouth.

Under normal circumstances, Boomer would never even entertain the thought of smoking crack, but the high volume of coke that he had just sniffed had him feeling invincible. He took a deep pull and inhaled.

Fruit jumped up and threw his hands up. "Yo, you on some other shit right now, son. I ain't fucking with that shit. What are you doing?" Fruit asked as he shook his head in disgust. Boomer was so busy elevating to another level that he didn't even hear Fruit's words.

Fruit didn't want to be a part of what Boomer was about to get into, so he stormed out, regretting the past three days. All he could think about was getting made an example out of by Macy. Fruit grew up admiring Macy, and for him to be a part of robbing him really didn't sit well with him. On top of that, Boomer was completely wilding out and seemed to be losing his mind.

Fruit still felt high as he jumped into his car. Paranoia grew by the minute, and he decided to go pay Macy a visit and try to exonerate himself before he got in too deep.

Boomer, on the other hand, had just sold his soul to the devil. He loved the feeling that the new drug had given him, and karma was fast approaching.

Fruit sped down the highway, swerving in and out of lanes as he made his way toward Macy's home. He rehearsed what he would say to Macy and had gone over it in his mind dozens of times. He actually thought that Macy would appreciate the fact that he would rat out Boomer. Fruit didn't want to feel the wrath of Macy, and he was about to try like hell to save his own ass.

Fruit pulled into the Sigel estate and quickly pulled in the driveway and hopped out. A guard stood outside and quickly went to the car when Fruit pulled up, stopping him in his tracks.

"Hold up, li'l nigga," the guard said as he put his hand on Fruit's chest.

"Get yo' fucking hands off of me. I need to holla at Macy!" Fruit said as he pushed the guard's hand off of him. Another guard heard the yelling and headed toward them.

"Don't get shot!" the guard threatened as he walked up on Fruit and put him in a full nelson. Fruit was slim-built, so he was no match as he got manhandled. One of the guards gave him a shot to the gut, making him bend over in pain as he clutched his stomach.

"I . . . just need to . . . see Macy," Fruit pleaded as he knelt down on one knee and breathed heavily.

Macy heard the chaos and stepped outside and saw Fruit. "Help him up!" Macy ordered as he slid his hand in his pocket and looked around, hoping to see Boomer. "Are you alone?" Macy asked as he frowned up.

"Yeah, but I know where Boomer is at," Fruit said as he stood up and winced from the pain.

"Step in, young man," Macy said calmly as he took a glance around and reentered the house.

Fruit mugged the guards and then proceeded to follow Macy into the house.

Macy didn't waste any time. "You got something to tell me?" Macy asked as he went for his glass jar of Scotch and poured himself a shot. Macy patiently waited for a response as he handed Fruit a shot of liquor. Fruit accepted the glass and Macy noticed that Fruit's hand shook nervously as he put the glass to his lips, trying to seem as if he was calm. Macy knew at that moment that Fruit had something to do with the robbery.

"That nigga is out of control. I tried to tell him not to do the shit, but he wouldn't listen," Fruit said as his voice shook in fear. Macy's presence was one of power, and it seemed to reek off of him like expensive cologne.

Macy clenched his teeth and his body began to sweat as Fruit confirmed what he had already known. Macy knew that Boomer was behind the robbery for sure, and that only added fuel to the fire as his trigger finger began to itch. Although he was the city's mayor, he still had his hustler's instinct.

Macy played it cool and didn't show his cards because he had to find out where his money was. "Where is Boomer and where is my money?" Macy asked calmly but firmly.

Fruit downed the rest of the drink and took a deep breath. He couldn't believe that he was ratting out his friend, but the fact that Boomer was smoking crack and living life on the edge made Fruit not want to be a part of an inevitable bad ending.

"I'm not a snitch or anything . . . but that nigga is wildin'," Fruit said. He was convincing himself that he wasn't being disloyal to his friend. He took another deep breath and continued. "He's staying at the Hilton. Room three-thirty," Fruit said as he pulled out a room key and handed it to Macy.

"Are you sure, son?" Macy said as he slightly frowned and looked deep into Fruit's eyes, trying to feel him out.

"Yeah, I'm sure. I just left him about a half an hour ago."

"You know if you are lying to me . . ." Macy said as he stepped closer to Fruit and placed his hand on his shoulder. Macy continued, "If you are lying to me, I will kill you. Believe that," Macy said as his gangster mentality began to rear its ugly head.

"I wouldn't lie to you, Mr. Sigel. He's in there and the money is there too," Fruit confessed as his heart began to pound. He saw the menacing stare in Macy's eyes and he grew uncomfortable standing in his presence.

Macy quickly walked to the door and waved for his bodyguard Big E to come in. E quickly came in, and Macy leaned over and whispered something in Edris' ear while Fruit stood and watched, not knowing what to expect next. Macy then walked over to Fruit and put his arm around him.

"Thanks for what you did. I will never forget this," Macy said as he walked Fruit toward the back.

"So there is no bad blood between us?" Fruit said, slightly surprised by Macy's reaction.

"No. None whatsoever. Actually, I owe you a favor. Maybe I can give you a job or something," Macy said as he patted his back.

No quicker had the words left his mouth than a bullet left his bodyguard's gun. The guard had walked behind Fruit and gave him a fatal blast to the head. Blood splattered everywhere as his body fell to the ground.

Macy wiped the blood off of his face and looked down at Fruit, who was still breathing. Macy looked at Edris and said, "Yo, give me that."

Edris followed his orders, and then Macy sent two more shots to Fruit's head, silencing him forever. Macy then spit on his body. He was tired of playing games, and he was in rare form. Stealing from him was a no-no, and Fruit had just learned the hard way.

"Clean this mess up and have this disappear before I get back. Fatima will be here in a minute, so make it quick," Macy instructed as he tucked the gun in his waist and headed out the door. He was on his way to pay Boomer a surprise visit.

Boomer lay in the bed and stared at the ceiling fan as it slowly spun. The hooker had just given him the best blowjob known to man, and he was in a daze. His mind raced in circles as he thought about nothing in particular. The drugs had him stuck and unable to move, and he never expected what was about to happen.

The lamp that once sat on the nightstand came crashing down on his head and dazed him. The hooker stood over him and moved frantically as she gathered all of the money that was spread on the bed and floor, putting it in the duffle bag with the other cash. She had decided to rob him once she found out how much money he had.

Her pimp was downstairs waiting outside for her. She had slipped in the bathroom and told him what caper she had stumbled upon, and he put the idea in her head. She waited for the right time and gave Boomer the business, knocking him nearly unconscious.

Boomer moaned and held his head as he saw nothing but stars. The hooker gathered her belongings and the duffle bag just before darting out of the room, leaving Boomer there alone. Boomer staggered to get up but fell right back down, not able to regain his balance.

"No, no, no," he moaned as he realized what had just happened. He grabbed the bed and used it as a crutch to get himself to his feet. He grabbed his gun from the nightstand, but once again he fell straight on his ass. He tried for a third time to get up, and the third time worked like a charm and he slowly walked to the door.

Just as he touched the door handle, the door swung open and Macy, along with two of his bodyguards, barged in. The guards rushed to Boomer, relieving him of his gun and holding him up for Macy to punch him. Macy's bodyguards were all ex-goons, so they were built for situations like that. Macy rolled up his sleeves and gave Boomer a hard punch to the gut, making him bend over in pain.

"You stole from me? Nigga, I raised you! Look at you. You high as ever! Off my money!" Macy said as his rage took over. All Macy saw was red, and he was steaming mad the more he thought about Boomer's audacity.

Boomer felt like a ton of bricks had hit him as he thought about who was standing in front of him.

"Where my money?" Macy asked as he scanned around the room, only seeing small piles of coke on the tables.

"She took it. The girl took it all," Boomer said as he swayed back and forth in agony.

"Who took it? What girl?" Macy asked as he frowned up and tried to figure out what Boomer was talking about.

"The bitch that I had in here. She hit me over the head and jacked the money," Boomer answered.

"Where the bitch at? Huh! Boomer, answer me!" Macy spat.

"I don't know. She ran out of here about five minutes ago," Boomer said as he breathed hard, trying to catch his wind.

"Don't fucking play with me. You better find that bitch, or the police going to find you on the side of the road slumped," Macy stated. "I want my damn money."

"Okay, okay. I will find her," Boomer said, trying to get out of the sticky situation.

"You better find her!" Macy said as he pointed his finger in Boomer's face. "You need to get yourself together and go see your mother. She worried about your sorry ass," Macy said as he fixed his collar and signaled for the guards to turn Boomer loose. The guards unleashed their grip on him and headed toward the exit.

"I want my damn money by tomorrow morning!" Macy said as he approached the door, preparing to exit.

Boomer's ego got the best of him as he burned up inside, thinking about how Macy was talking to him like he was a flunky. In his mind, he was a boss, and the thought of being disrespected was too much to let slide. Maybe the cocaine had him braver than usual. Nevertheless, Boomer couldn't help himself; he had to say something.

"I'll have your money," Boomer said as he stood up and wiped the blood that trickled from his forehead. "Bitch," he added, to add insult to injury.

He would forever regret those words. That single word sent Macy over the edge, and he turned around, drew his gun, and put a hollow tip through Boomer's head. Macy didn't even think twice about what he had just done.

Just as quickly as rage had entered Macy's mind, guilt crept in. As he saw his son lying on the floor staring into space, he began to think about Fatima. Fatima and Boomer shared the same eyes, and that was the hardest thing he had ever done. But he knew that if he didn't do it, Boomer would have eventually killed him. Boomer's hate for Macy was deep, and it wasn't a secret.

The guards were totally taken off guard by Macy's actions, never thinking that he would or could kill his own son. Macy slowly knelt down and gently kissed Boomer on the forehead. He then ran his hand over Boomer's face so that he could close the eyes that seemed to be staring directly at him. Macy had just done something that he could never take back.

Macy knew that he was slipping. He was moving so sloppy and jeopardizing his entire life over money. He had never shed a tear in his adult life, but as he sat parked in his driveway, watching his wife's silhouette as she moved around in the upstairs window, he cried. Silent tears ran down his face as he thought of how he had singlehandedly ripped his family apart. He had killed his son, and despite the fact that Boomer was in the wrong, Macy was far from right.

Macy was usually a calm and collected man. He barely moved if his actions weren't strategic or well thought out. Everything that had occurred since his anniversary dinner was chaotic, sporadic . . . stupid. He hit his steering wheel, wishing that he could take back the past hour of his life. Dazed, he watched his wife's shadow move around their room.

"I can't go in there right now," he said aloud, knowing that when he looked into her eyes, he would see Boomer staring back at him. He pulled out and immediately called Edris.

"Everything's in order," Edris stated as soon as he picked up the phone. "I cleaned up that mess. Fatima will never know anything."

Macy stopped him. "I fucked up. I need you to meet me at my office."

"Yeah, I'm on my way," Edris stated as he looked over to ensure that his wife was fully asleep.

"Bring me a change of clothes and hurry, E. It's important," Macy said.

Macy sat with his executive leather chair turned toward the floor-to-ceiling windows. He was deep in thought when he heard Edris enter the room.

"The clothes will be a little big, but they should fit okay," Edris stated as he stepped toward the desk. He had no idea why Macy needed the clothing, but he had learned a long time ago not to ask questions.

Macy turned around, and Edris' eyes bugged out as he noticed the blood that stained his slacks and shirt.

"I found Boom," Macy stated.

"What did you do, boss?" Edris asked. He could tell that things had gone bad. Macy's red eyes and solemn demeanor told Edris so. "What did you do?"

"I snapped," Macy replied in a low tone. "I fucked up. I forgot who he was, and I just snapped." Macy knew that if he was in his right frame of mind, he would have never killed Boomer, but anger was like a drug to him. He was never clear when pushed to the edge.

"I can't tell Fatima this. She will never forgive me for this. He was our son. . . . He was family."

Macy shook his head and looked at Big E. "I need you to get that tape from the hotel. I was messy. I slipped out of an emergency exit after I shot Boomer. I can't be tied to this murder. Housekeeping doesn't come around until ten, so they won't discover the body until morning. After that the police will be knocking on my door. No one can know that I was anywhere near that hotel. If they ask, I was with you tonight. We were here at the office working late. Without the surveillance video, no one will ever suspect me of killing my own son."

Edris nodded. He was speechless and in utter disbelief that Macy had taken it to this point. He had witnessed the tension firsthand between the father and son duo. Boomer had been a problem child since he hit puberty, rebelling every chance that he could. Macy had pegged it as teenage rebellion, until the drug use entered the picture.

"You all right?" Edris asked.

Macy nodded his head and reached into his desk. He removed a large yellow envelope filled with money. He tossed it on the desk toward Edris. "When you get that tape, I'll be fine," he replied.

***

Edris entered the hotel and walked directly up to the desk clerk. The young Asian girl flipped carelessly through a magazine as she worked the night shift.

"I'm sorry, we don't have any availability. All of our rooms are reserved for the night," she said without looking up.

Edris leaned into the counter. "I'm not here for a room." He went into the inside pocket of his pea coat and pulled out the money-filled envelope. He placed it on the counter and slid it to the girl.

"What's this?" she asked as she grabbed the envelope.

"Take a look inside," he urged.

The girl opened the envelope, and when she saw all of the Ben Franklins staring back at her, she dropped it as if it were hot to the touch.

She leaned over the counter, and her chinky eyes peered at him suspiciously. "What is this?"

"It can be yours if you cooperate," Edris responded. Macy had already acted irrationally, and Boomer's murder was going to blow up the spot. Edris couldn't bring more conflict to the situation. It was sometimes more effective to put a little sugar in the game, as opposed to shit. He was going to sweeten the pot for the young girl so that she would help him cover up Boomer's murder.

"Cooperate how? I don't understand what you want from me," the girl replied with a slight tremor in her voice.

"Relax, sweetheart. If I wanted to hurt you, you would have never seen me coming. I just want to talk. You understand?" Edris asked. "Can we talk?"

She nodded her head, still nervous as she looked around the empty lobby. She had no choice but to hear

Edris out because there was no one in sight, in case she needed help.

"Now, something happened inside this hotel tonight, and I need the surveillance tapes," Edris stated. "How much would I have to give you for you to give me the tapes and forget that you ever saw me?"

"I . . . I . . ." The girl stammered, unsure of what to say or even what number to throw out.

"I'm trying to talk business with you, baby girl, so just calm down and put your big girl panties on," Edris stated. "What's your price?"

The girl knew that she could be fired for even thinking about giving over the tapes, but she had a feeling that this could be a bigger payday than she would ever see in a week's check. She thought of all the bills that were stacking up at her house and of the college tuition that was due in a few weeks. "Five thousand dollars," she said, feeling as if she were reaching. The girl never expected Edris to pay her that much money for one measly tape, but she had no clue who she was dealing with. Edris did not immediately respond, and she was worried that she had gone too high.

"If that's too high . . ."

"There is twenty thousand dollars in that envelope. You can have it for the tapes and for you to forget about this little conversation," Edris proposed.

The girl slid the envelope behind the desk and was too excited to contain the sly smile that spread across her thin lips. "What conversation?" she asked.

Edris chuckled and nodded his head. "My girl. Now, the shit is going to hit the fan soon, and when it does, you don't know shit and you didn't see shit," Edris schooled. "Now, show me where the surveillance is."

The girl led him to the back, where the recording system was set up. Edris had the girl leave him alone, because he did not want her to notice Macy's face on the tapes. He didn't need her looking over his shoulders. He ran the tapes back and watched as Macy walked through the lobby and up to Boomer's room. He could only imagine what had gone down inside. He immediately popped the tape out of the recorder and then erased the data on the system for the entire day. He pocketed the tape and then emerged from the room.

"Give me your license," he told the girl.

"What?" she questioned.

"For insurance. You will be completely safe as long as you keep up your end of the deal. If you talk about this to anybody, especially the police, I'll know where to find you, and I'ma come see you. My next visit won't be so friendly," he warned.

The girl removed her license with hesitance. She made a copy of it behind the desk and slid him the copy. "I won't say a word."

He folded the paper and put it in his pocket with the tape and replied, "You better not."

He walked out of the hotel like a ghost. It was the first and last time that the place would ever see him.

Chapter Seven

Fatima lay in bed restlessly as her mind spun uncontrollably. It had been two days since she had spoken to Boomer, and she wished that he would just come home.

"What if something happened to him?" Fatima asked as she turned to face Macy, who was reading a copy of *Black Enterprise*, catching up on his finances before he went to bed.

Macy heard her question but acted as if he were too distracted to respond. Guilt filled him because he knew that she was waiting for a child who was never coming home again. He wanted to tell her what had happened, but she would never understand. He knew that Fatima's love for her son outweighed any love she had for anyone else, even herself. He could never let her find out that he was behind Boomer's death. It was a wrath that he knew he did not want to see.

"Macy?" she whined.

He looked up from his reading and saw the apprehensive look on her face. Her tired, red eyes revealed her worry, and she looked as if she had aged five years overnight. He reached over and pulled her near him so that she was snuggled against his body, resting her head on his chest.

"You said he was high when you spoke with him, right?" Macy asked.

"Yeah, but—"

"Don't panic, Tima. You know how Boomer gets when he goes on his binges," Macy said as he rubbed her hair gently. "He'll turn up. Don't stress out over this."

"You're probably right," she whispered as she shook her head. "I can tell you this: If he is okay, I'm going to kill him when I finally see him. He can't keep doing this to me. The drugs and the recklessness, it all has to stop. He's my baby, and I can't be up worrying over him like this. He has to get help. Macy, you have to help him. He loves you and he looks up to you."

Her words penetrated his heart, and he felt a small pain in his chest. "I will, baby. Get some sleep," he said, his voice breaking slightly as he kissed the top of her head. He folded the magazine in his hands and reached over to the nightstand to turn off the lamp. The darkness helped conceal the sin he had committed. He didn't know if he could keep up his lie if he had to see how badly Fatima was hurting.

The doorbell rang, and Fatima shot up, throwing the covers off of her body. "That's him!" she assumed, knowing that no one else could be at the front door at 2:00 A.M.

She threw on her short silk kimono robe. Macy was barely out of bed before she was racing down the stairs to answer the door. She snatched open the door, and her anxious face fell in horror when she saw the two police officers standing before her.

"Hello, Mrs. Sigel," one of the officers greeted. His tone was respectful, and even though she didn't know him, the officer was well aware of who she was. As the mayor's wife, she was very well known throughout the city.

"Officers," she said back. "Can I help you?" she asked as she tightened her robe.

Macy finally came down the stairs and stood by her side. He put his hand on the small of her back. "Jamison, Williams," he greeted as he reached out to shake the young men's hands while calling them by name. "Please come inside."

They stepped into the foyer and hesitantly directed their attention toward Macy.

"Mr. Mayor . . . um, we . . . we're here about your son."

Fatima's heart sank when she heard those words. "No . . . no . . ." she whispered, already knowing the news that they were about to deliver.

"I'm sorry to deliver the news that he has been murdered."

"No! Macy, no!" Fatima shouted as pain took over her entire body. The wind was knocked out of her, and she doubled over as if she had been punched in the abdomen. She gripped her stomach as she let out an animalistic howl. "No! My baby!" She broke down, not caring that she had an audience.

Macy went to her side, and she collapsed into him as she cried her eyes out on his shoulder. "I'm so sorry, Tima. I'm sorry, baby," he whispered. She didn't know the true meaning of his words, but he was apologizing because the burden of Boomer's death rested on his shoulders. He was the one who had pulled the trigger, and now he was forced to watch his wife fall apart.

"Thank you, gentlemen. Please see yourselves out," Macy said without ever letting Fatimah go. She was hysterical and so weak at the knees that if he let her go, she would hit the floor.

"When you get a chance, we need one of you to come and view the body to confirm that it's him," the officer said in a low, hesitant tone.

Macy nodded, and the officers left as Macy catered to his wife.

Fatima could hardly contain herself; she was sobbing so hard. "Oh my God. . . . Macy, he's dead," she screamed sorrowfully.

"Shhh, it's okay. I'm going to take care of you, ma. Shhh, everything is going to be okay," he whispered as he tried to soothe her. He had known that she would react this way, but seeing it made his conscience heavy.

The two of them had never had any secrets between them, but Macy's actions had polluted their relationship. This was a secret that he could never tell her because he knew that she would never understand. Forgiveness for this act was something that Fatima would never lend him, and as he held her tightly, he told himself that he could never let her find out. Boomer's murder would be something that he took to his grave.

Fatima went numb after they identified the body. Seeing her only child lying so stiff in the city morgue killed her. It was as if a vital part of her had died right along with Boomer. She completely withdrew inside of herself and allowed Macy to take the lead. She didn't make one funeral arrangement. Macy planned everything and spared no expense. Fatima appreciated Macy because he held her up in front of the cameras and the crowd. He would send Boomer home with class and style, ensuring that the last memory that people got of him was a positive one. What she thought he did out of love was really out of pure guilt.

Macy tried desperately to pull Fatima out of her funk. He needed her to be at her best at all times, and Boomer's death was taking a hefty toll on her. A great sadness had taken over her spirit.

Boomer's death was nothing but bad press for Macy. As an elected official in the city, people were having a field day and labeling him as a man who had strong ties with L.A.'s most notorious drug dealers and gang leaders. Things grew increasingly tense as he tried to maintain a good image. Everything had to be carefully calculated. He couldn't make any spontaneous moves without it being scrutinized. Not only were his policies in jeopardy, so was his character, and the last thing Macy needed was this unwanted attention.

He was well aware that he had brought it upon himself, and he tried everything to right his wrongs, but it was useless. Fatima was completely torn up over Boomer's death, and the lady who usually made him look good could barely even hold herself together. All of the chaos had been a direct result of Macy's stupid actions. *I should have never gone to see Boomer with a pistol on my hip,* Macy thought with regret.

Los Angeles was a city that would build you up just to tear you down, and Macy was feeling the pressure. He had set himself up to win, and all of the cards had been stacked in his favor until Boomer had deviated from the plan. Boomer was the only piece of his puzzle that didn't fit. He wasn't a part of Macy's American dream. His drug addiction and reckless behavior had made him the bad seed in the family. The way that Boomer was living, Macy knew that one day Boomer would become a problem. Never in a million years did he expect to be the one to rock him to sleep.

As Macy stared out of the window of his office he shook his head, hoping that the entire situation would become yesterday's news sooner rather than later.

"When are these mu'fuckas going to move on from this?" he asked rhetorically.

Big E, who sat across from Macy's executive desk, shrugged his shoulders and replied, "I don't know, but the longer they linger on it, the more attention they bring to it. That means the spotlight and all eyes are resting on you right now."

"That's a problem," Macy said in a low voice. "We still have people on payroll inside of the police force, right?"

Macy hadn't wanted to grease political palms or make friends before, but he was glad that he had. The connections that he had been hesitant about making were the same ones that were going to save his ass.

"Yeah, they are in place," Edris responded.

"Good. I need Boomer's murder buried. This can't get out," he whispered.

Macy realized what was on the line; not only was his freedom in jeopardy, but also his marriage. Everything he had done to get to this level of success would be in vain if it was all taken away because of Boomer.

He closed his blinds and turned toward Big E. "Make sure this goes away as soon as possible, and I want those fucking news vans off of this property," he snapped.

Macy watched from the window as Edris went and did his job, ensuring that no one got into the building who wasn't employed there. He couldn't allow this situation to get out of hand. It was containable at the moment, but Macy knew that one more negative encounter was all that was needed to send his world spiraling downward.

It wasn't the act of murder that disturbed Macy. He had put in work before, and he understood what came along with taking the life of another. But this one had not been planned, and it hit close to home because it was the biggest mistake that he had ever made.

As he watched the media pack up their things and drive away in their TV news vans, he sighed in relief. Macy just hoped that this would not escalate because he truly believed in karma, and after the sin that he had committed, he knew that nothing good could lie in his dismal future.

The seams to his life seemed to be coming undone, and with Fatima devastated over Boomer's untimely death, she was no longer the glue that held everything together. As a couple they had never been so vulnerable, and as a man, Macy had never felt so low.

What type of man does that to the child he raised? he thought somberly. He remembered teaching Boomer to ride a bike. It was Macy who had stayed up with Boomer teaching him the ins and outs of sports as they watched different games together. Before Boomer began experimenting with narcotics, the two had been close, but that seemed so long ago. The world had corrupted things too much to go back to those happier times, and whether he wanted to admit it or not, things would never be the same.

Chapter Eight

It was the day of Boomer's funeral service. The cemetery yard was packed, and cloudy skies loomed over the city on that day. Macy's bodyguards acted as pallbearers as they carried the silver-plated casket to the burial site. Supporters and family friends gathered around the rectangular dugout that would be Boomer's final resting place.

Macy stood next to his wife, consoling her as she cried in his arms. They both were draped in all black, mourning the death of their loved one. Macy had mixed emotions and began to regret what he did after seeing the pain and suffering his wife had endured because of his spontaneous action. Macy's conscience was getting the best of him because every time he looked at his wife, he saw Boomer.

As the casket was set on the foundation, preparing for it to be lowered into the ground, the spectators looked on as the preacher began the sermon.

Damn, Boomer. Why did you have to do this to yourself? Macy thought as he shook his head in shame. A veteran of the street game and having past experience with people who held envy in their heart, Macy knew that if he didn't kill Boomer when he did, Boomer would have eventually done him in. Macy regretted it, but it was necessary.

As the preacher finished up the sermon, a slightly heavyset lady with a big black hat stepped out of the crowd. A soulful voice emerged from her vocal cords as she began to sing her own rendition of "A Change Is Gonna Come." It seemed as if her voice was touched by the angels, and her song only ignited more tears within the audience.

As she sang, the casket was slowly being lowered, and that was when Fatima lost it. Her knees buckled, and Macy had to catch her from falling.

"I got you, baby," he whispered into her ear as he held her up. As he looked at his wife falling apart, he really contemplated resigning as mayor. He began to question his choices in life. Here he was, a real street nigga in a political realm. He didn't fit in and he knew it. No matter how many fancy suits or rich friends he had, he still was a boy from the ghetto. The only difference was that he made it out. However, you can take the boy out of the ghetto, but not the ghetto out of the boy. Macy knew that the hood mentality was still in him, and burying Boomer was the proof.

Light rain began to fall, and while other people assumed that it was just an act of Mother Nature, Macy knew that it was tears of the late Boomer.

Meanwhile, Case was on the other side, itching to get to Macy. He had always had a slight jealousy issue with Macy. He believed that Macy purposely kept him underneath him and stunted his growth in the drug game. He believed Case only gave him a chance to grow once he himself was out of the drug game. Case didn't understand that it wasn't Macy keeping him from growing, but his own brute approach and lack of business skills.

The birth of the green-eyed monster that society calls jealousy came into play years ago. It was when Macy didn't allow Case to meet the out-of-town coke connect. Case always believed that he and Macy were equal partners until that day. Case could remember it like it was yesterday. . . .

It was the year of 1998, and crack had just reached full stride in the black community. Macy and his squad of goons had the whole city on lock and afraid. He ran a flawless operation with over fifteen operating crack houses within the city. Macy was virtually unstoppable. Macy was what you called a people's champ. The community embraced him even though he was the one responsible for tearing it down.At the time, Case was Macy's head street general and mostly handled all of the dirty work for him.

Friends since childhood, they had a bond, and both played an integral part in the operation. Macy was the brains and Case was the muscle. They both understood their role and everything was smooth, but as the old saying goes, once envy enters, reason leaves. This was a prime example of that saying, and it didn't show up until Macy was on his way to Florida to visit his coke connection.

Macy suavely looked at his watch and then slid his hand into his right pocket. He was standing in line so that he could go through the security checkpoint. His heart beat fast as his adrenaline began to pick up. He wasn't usually the nervous type, but with $150,000 of unreported cash in his briefcase, it made him uneasy, and rightfully so. He stood in line as the security guards stood by the metal detector. A bead of sweat dripped from his brow, and he hoped like hell that he wasn't going to be a subject for a random search.

He usually would have sent a female to make the run for him, but that weekend was a special one. His coke connect had finally agreed to meet him face to face.

The connect was a man by the name of Carter Diamond, who was well associated with a Dominican supplier. Macy had been dealing with a third party for the past two summers, and finally the connect wanted to meet the man who bought ten bricks or more from him every month. It was a common courtesy. Macy saw the bigger picture and knew that by meeting the coke connect, his prices would go down. The fewer hands the cocaine traveled through, the purer the product and the cheaper the price.

Macy smiled as he thought about the opportunity that was in front of him. He slid past the metal detector and guards without a problem and took a deep breath once he got a few yards away. He quickly made his way over to a pay phone so that he could phone Case to make sure he was on his way driving down to Miami. Because Macy couldn't travel with guns, he ordered Case to meet him in Miami by car.

Macy placed the briefcase by his feet, and he attempted to make a call on the pay phone. He slid his back to the phone as he placed the receiver to his ear. He wanted to make sure everything was going as planned.

Macy confirmed that Case had arrived and hung up the phone. He only had an hour before he was supposed to be meeting with the infamous Carter Diamond. Carter was notorious and one of the richest hustlers in the game. He was an extraordinary businessman on top of being a supplier of large quantities of blow. This was what set him away from the pack. He married into a cocaine family and got instantly plugged.

Macy walked outside the airport and waited for a limo to pick him up, compliments of Carter Diamond. The limo pulled off, and Macy got to ride through the city of Miami for the very first time—the city where the crime family "The Cartel" ruled.

After a thirty-minute ride, the limo pulled up to a gigantic mansion that was surrounded by tall steel gates. The beautiful home sat on an estate—the Diamond estate, to be exact. Macy couldn't believe he was about to visit the home of the biggest drug lord North America had ever seen.

Macy was young, but he had an old soul, which enabled him to move up in the ranks and gain control of the streets; but he never thought that it would get him to this level. Butterflies formed in his stomach as the driver rolled down his window to show his face for entry. As they bypassed the gates, Macy noticed that Carter had armed men around his fence, and he was taking notes. He wanted to handle his operation just as his connect was—with power and security.

They pulled up to the wrap-around driveway and parked. Macy was let out by the driver. He then escorted him around the house to the back, where the pool was located. The back was immaculate. The pool was shaped like a diamond, and the flowers around the yards were exotic and colorful, only adding to the beautiful view. The sound of laughter and water splashing filled the air as Macy noticed a couple kids playing in the water. Macy looked down at the yard and had not seen grass so green his entire life.

The driver stopped in his tracks and placed his hand on the shoulder of Macy. "Mr. Diamond is waiting for you just ahead," he said in his deep and raspy voice.

"Thank you," Macy said in a low tone as he nodded his head in acknowledgment.

Macy noticed a man sitting at the pool with an open linen shirt and linen pants. He also sipped on a glass of cognac on ice as he watched the young kids play in the pool. Macy immediately knew who the man was; it was Carter Diamond.

As Macy approached the man, his heart began to beat harder and harder. He was far from scared, but the feeling of anxiety overcame him. Carter stood up and extended his hand as Macy approached.

"How was your trip?" Carter asked as he firmly shook the hand of his guest.

"Good, good," Macy answered.

"Have a seat," Carter suggested as he waved at the chair at the table. Macy took a seat and Carter did also.

Carter looked into the eyes of the up-and-coming hustler he had sent for. "So you're the man that can move bricks like magic, huh?" Carter said as he took a pull of his cigar.

"I guess you can say that," Macy answered as a smile formed on his face.

Carter looked into Macy's eyes and tried to read him. He wanted to see if there was any fear or hesitation evident. However, Carter could sense no trace of fear whatsoever. If he really knew that Macy was nervous, he would have ended the meeting right then and there. Carter liked to have strong people around him, and being timid would have gotten Macy a first-class ticket back home.

"I have been watching you for some time now. Not to startle you, but it's just the truth. I sent my goons down there to see what was going on. I thought to myself, how does the young black man move so much weight? He has to be a fed, I said to myself. But shit, you just a natural-born hustler," Carter said just before he took a puff of his cigar.

Two young boys began to tussle near the poolside and took Carter's attention off of Macy. "Hey, hey! Mecca and Monroe, stop fighting each other!" Carter yelled as he gave the two young boys a stern look. They quickly stopped at the sound of their father's voice, and Carter focused his attention back on Macy. "Sorry about that. My boys are kind of rough," Carter said proudly.

"Yeah, I see," Macy said as he glanced over at the half-black, half-Dominican twin boys.

"Look, I invited you out here where I rest my head. As you can see, I am a family man. I really see potential in you. I don't open my home to just anybody, and I want you to know that."

"I appreciate the gesture," Macy said as a waiter came and poured him a glass of cognac. Macy nodded and took a sip of the liquor.

"Okay, let's get to business. I am willing to give you as many bricks as you can handle—on consignment. However, your man . . . I don't like the way he moves," Carter said as his smile turned upside down, signaling that he was dead serious.

"I don't understand," Macy answered, trying to figure out Carter's angle.

"Follow me. Let's go inside," Carter said as he stood up. Macy's mind began to race, wondering what exactly Carter was getting at. However, he stood and followed Carter as he headed to the beach house that was a few yards away.

"Like I said, my men have been watching you for some time. I got word that he is a hothead and tends to be flashy. Those are two traits that a good drug dealer doesn't need to have. Do you know how to spell flashy?" Carter asked as they walked side by side. "F-E-D-S," he stated before Macy could get a chance to respond.

They stepped into the pool house, where a man was waiting for them.

"This is my right-hand man, Polo," Carter said as he nodded his head toward Polo. Macy and Polo nodded at each other in acknowledgment, and a cold, intense look was in Polo's eyes. Macy didn't back down and returned the glare without an ounce of fear.

Carter broke the tension by suggesting that they go downstairs. Macy looked around confused. It was a small room, and no stairs to even offer a downstairs existed.

Carter smoothly walked over to the bookshelf and pulled a book that was actually a hidden lever. Almost immediately a portion of the wall slid over, revealing a secret passage.

"Follow me, gentlemen," Carter said as he headed down.

Macy tried not to have a surprised look and kept his ice grill, but nevertheless, he was impressed. He had never seen anything like it before. It was like a scene straight out of a movie.

They all went down the stairs where the sound of Miles Davis was playing and the room was dimly lit. The stairs and floors were carpeted with a deep red color and it seemed more like a lair than a basement. It was a relaxing setting, but that soon changed when Macy noticed the man who sat bound to a chair. The man had a potato bag over his head and was squirming, trying to free himself.

"What the fuck?" Macy asked as he looked at Carter, who had a slight grin on his face.

Polo walked over to the man and pulled out a handgun. He placed the gun to the squirming man's head and looked at Carter. Carter then looked at Macy and began to speak.

"This is you right-hand man, Case. I had one of my goons snatch him up from the hotel room where he was waiting for you at. You have a choice. I am only going to ask you this one time, so listen close. If you make the decision right now to off your man, you have my word that you will be connected for life. You will have grade-A coke and my political connections. You will virtually be transformed to a kingpin overnight," Carter carefully said. He made sure Macy understood every single word that escaped his mouth.

Macy was totally taken off guard and stared at his friend, who was sitting before him. Macy was a man before anything, and he let Carter know.

"I stand behind my nigga. If he has to die for me to get connected, then it's not worth it. If you shoot him, you might as well shoot me right," Macy said bravely as he looked Carter square in the eye.

Carter nodded his head in approval and grinned slightly. He knew at that moment that he had picked the right protégé.

Polo also grinned, impressed with Carter's judge of character. Polo then snatched the sack off of the man's head, revealing his face. Macy gasped in disbelief. The man wasn't Case, but a guy he had never seen before. A sock was stuffed in his mouth, and he was already beaten badly; Macy could tell by the bloody nose and two black eyes.

"What the fuck is going on?" Macy asked Carter, as he was totally puzzled.

"That was just a test. I knew that if you were willing to cross your own man, then down the line you would eventually cross me. I respect your gangster, young blood. I respect it," Carter said as he slowly nodded his head up and down in approval.

Macy smiled, realizing that he was dealing with some serious gangsters and was happy to be in their circle. He then asked out of curiosity, "So who is this?" he said as he pointed at the man tied up.

"This is the nigga's place you are taking. Come to find out, he was talking to the feds. Ain't that a bitch?" Carter said as he reached for the gun that Polo held.

"So what you going to do with him? Kill him?" Macy asked.

"No, not at all. I'm a businessman. I'm not a killer," Carter said as he took a step closer to Macy. "You are going to kill him," Carter said as he handed Macy the loaded weapon. Carter was testing Macy's gangster and also verifying that he wasn't an undercover. He knew that if he was a cop, he wouldn't kill a man.

Macy, young and ambitious, took the gun and gave the man two to the head without hesitation. Not one of them even flinched as the loud shots rang out. On that day, it was solidified that Macy was connected.

When Macy went to explain the ordeal to Case, Case wondered why he wasn't invited, and that was the beginning of the end.

Chapter Nine

The weeks following Boomer's death were one big blur to Fatima. She could hardly remember if she was coming or going her head was in such disarray. She couldn't focus on anything, and it felt as if she had a gaping hole where her heart used to be. Pinot Grigio became her escape and her only confidant. She lived in a constant state of inebriation to avoid dealing with Boomer's death. She silently blamed herself. She had been so preoccupied with her own life, so busy and involved with Macy's political career. Now with Boomer gone she was forced to admit that she had contributed to his destructive lifestyle.

I saw him falling apart. If I would have been more focused on him, this would not have happened. I should have gotten him off the drugs, she thought somberly. Hindsight was always 20/20, and she wished that she could go back and right her past's wrongs.

Macy could see Fatima falling into a depression. He was going above and beyond to pull her out of it, but his efforts were futile. Nothing could shake the hazy fog that had fallen over her. She couldn't see through all of the pain. She slept days away to avoid dealing with reality. Her world had become too chaotic to even cope with. Although she was well aware of Boomer's drug issues, she still could not believe that he was gone. The police had labeled his homicide drug related, which meant that he would just become another unsolved murder.

As Macy entered the room, he saw Fatima lying on the bed with her hands tucked safely between her thighs. He could tell from the rhythm of her breathing that she wasn't asleep. He knew her like the back of his hand and didn't even have to ask what she was thinking of.

"Stop obsessing over this, Tima. He's gone. There is nothing that anyone can do to bring Boomer back," Macy said as he stood over her.

"I know. I would just feel better if I knew who killed him and why," Fatima said.

"You don't want to know that," Macy replied surely. "Just let it go."

Fatima looked past him and out of the window. She was so absent and distant that Macy was willing to do anything to snap her out of it.

"You can't just rot away in this house, ma," he whispered. "I'm worried about you, Tima. I've got meetings and stuff to attend, so I can't just look after you every minute of the day. Why don't you get dressed and get out of the house. Go shopping . . . on me . . . and afterwards, go check into a plush room, enjoy some time at the spa. Relax your mind and get your spirit right. You deserve it after what you've been through," Macy said as he reached into his suit jacket and removed his wallet. He pulled out a black card and placed it on the nightstand. "I know you're not going to turn that down."

For the first time in weeks, she laughed slightly, giving him a soft smile. "That's my girl," he said as he helped her out of the bed.

Fatima dressed quickly, and Macy checked on her before he left for the day. "You need me to call the car service for you?"

Fatima shook her head. "No. I can drive myself. I want to be alone anyway."

Macy's office phone rang loudly, and she nodded her head. "Go ahead. I'm fine, baby. I'm on my way out. I'll call you to check in," she said.

Macy kissed her cheek and retreated to answer his phone call as she headed out. She grabbed the keys to Macy's Mercedes, knowing that it had more trunk space for her purchases, and then pulled off.

Fatima wasn't a mall shopper, and with Macy's permission, she ripped through Rodeo Drive like a professional buyer. She indulged in everything from Mikimoto pearls to Fendi handbags, not even stopping long enough to look at a price tag. On any other day, this would have been her dream, a shopping spree with no limits and no man beside her to slow her down; but no matter how much stuff she purchased, she still felt low. Her spirit was dampened. The death of her son had damn near snuffed out any possibility of future happiness.

Her face had been plastered all over the news during her son's funeral. Macy's political career had made Boomer's death local news, and as she patronized her favorite stores, she could feel the curious eyes of the other customers. She was a recognizable figure around the city of Los Angeles, and it only made it harder to deal with the chaos. She needed solace and privacy so that she could process her loss in her own way. Oversized shades covered her swollen eyes as she spent a small fortune trying to make her sorrow go away.

It wasn't long before the media got wind of her outing, and soon cameras and reporters were crowding her. She maneuvered through the crowd of paparazzi and avoided their questions as she kept her head down.

"Mrs. Sigel, how are you dealing with the death of your son?" a reporter asked as she shoved a microphone in Fatima's face.

"Is it true that your son's death was drug related?" another asked.

"Is it true that the mayor is an affiliate of known drug dealers in the city? Is that why your son was shot and killed?"

Fatima pushed the microphones out of her face as she carried her packages to the car. The media were like vultures as they attacked her with a barrage of intrusive questions. She had learned long ago never to open her mouth for them. It wouldn't have mattered what she said; they would have twisted her words and spun a story to portray her in a negative light.

The city officials were already up in arms that Macy Sigel, a black man, was the elected mayor. She had to be extremely careful how she moved. She had to constantly be prepared to handle the press, which was why she said nothing and gave them the cold shoulder as she rushed to get in the car. Her shopping trip had been cut short, and it was on days like today that she felt like her lavish lifestyle was not worth the cost she paid to live it.

A mother deserves to deal with the death of her son in peace, she thought as a tear escaped from behind the glasses on her face. Through her jaded lens, all she could see was sadness. This had been the first day that she had felt a sense of normalcy return to her world, and in the blink of an eye, the news reporters had ruined it. The way that she was feeling, she was tempted to go off on them for being disrespectful and for turning her family's tragedy into the city's latest entertainment story. They were making her life appear to be a circus act on TV, and she was vexed. Fatima knew that she couldn't act out her anger, however. She had a husband to represent, and she had always done it well.

She popped the trunk and went to place her belongings inside. Fatima jumped slightly and paused as she snatched her arm back out of the trunk. Bloody clothes lay crumpled inside, and she quickly closed the trunk so that the prying paparazzi and reporters did not notice.

Where did those clothes come from? Why is Macy hiding them? she thought as a dull ache filled her. Her intuition was telling her that something wasn't right, and she quickly shook the cameras as she hit the expressway and headed out to the beach. It was where she went when she needed to think.

As she stepped out of her car, the smell of the salt water appealed to her. She quickly went into the trunk of the car and pulled out the bloody clothes. "He was wearing these the day Boomer died," she said with a gasp. "Why is there blood?" she asked.

Fatima wasn't naïve and didn't want to assume that Macy was clean-cut. He had always been hood and prominently respected in the drug game. Overall, he wasn't a good guy, but he was good to her. She didn't want to think that he would ever do anything to hurt her. A million and one thoughts went through her head as she gripped the clothes in her hand. *Don't assume anything. This could be anyone's blood,* she thought.

Fatima took off her expensive shoes and put the clothes in the back seat of her car before stepping onto the smooth sand. It sank between her toes as she began to walk down the beach as the sun set behind her. She picked up her phone to call Macy, but hung up quickly, knowing that the questions she had to ask were ones that needed to be asked in person.

***

Fatima walked into the house clutching the bloody clothes in her hand. She had already told herself that Macy would have a good explanation for hiding them in the trunk of his car, but she wanted to hear what he had to say. She wanted to see his face when she questioned him about them. Fatima silently prayed that his explanation made sense. She needed to hear him say something that made her feel silly for ever thinking otherwise. Fatima needed Macy to look her in the face and tell her that he had nothing to do with Boomer's death.

A nagging sensation gripped her as she stalked toward his office, determined yet nervous at the same time. Macy wasn't expecting her. At that moment, she was supposed to be an hour away, across town, enjoying a Swedish massage and sipping expensive champagne, but her mind wouldn't let this go.

She could hear voices coming from the back of the house, and she realized that Macy was not alone. She recognized Edris' voice and crept silently as she stood outside of the office door. Itching to confront Macy, she cursed under her breath because she would have to wait until his company left. Fatima didn't like to air her dirty laundry in the streets, and impatience ate away at her cool visage. She took a deep breath to calm herself and was about to announce her presence, until she heard her name come up.

"How's Tima doing with all of this?" Edris asked.

Fatima put her ear to the thick cherry wood door, ear-hustling as she tried to intercept the entire conversation.

"Not good at all, fam. She's broken over this shit," Macy revealed. "It's fucked up, because I'm sitting back watching her go through it."

"Does she have any idea that it was you?" Edris asked.

Fatima's heart fell, and she felt as if someone had snatched the air from her lungs. She hoped that she had heard it wrong, and she held her breath as she waited for Macy to respond.

"Nah, she doesn't know. It's all bad right now, though, fam. That shit is eating me up. Every day I'm looking her in her eyes knowing I killed Boomer. I've handled many niggas before, but Boomer is eating me alive," Macy admitted. "She's my wife, and I took a piece of her soul away. I don't think she will ever be the same."

Fatima's emotions overtook her as she stormed into the office. Anger, sadness, shock, pain . . . it all shot through her as she rushed Macy. She threw the bloody clothes at him. There was no need to question where they had come from. The brown stains were a brutal reflection of the crime that Macy had committed. It was Boomer's blood, and she felt as if she could not breathe as she attacked his killer.

"You bastard!" she shouted. Her nostrils flared. "You killed him! You killed my son?" she said, posing a question of disbelief.

Macy was taken off guard and was about to fix his mouth to deny her accusations, but she had heard it from his very lips. There was no lying his way out of it. She knew the truth, and as he tried to wrap his arms around her, he immediately sensed a change in her. Her body instantly went stiff as she stopped breathing.

Fatima didn't know if she was frozen in fear or if she was just stifling her anger. She could not believe what she had just overheard, and she just knew that her mind was playing tricks on her. But when she saw the expression of guilt on her husband's face, her stomach churned and she felt as if she would be sick. Fatima went ballistic.

"Don't touch me!" she shouted as she picked up the paperweight from his mahogany desk and tossed it at him. She swept the contents off of his desk, throwing anything that felt heavy enough to inflict harm. "Don't touch me!" she yelled again when Edris tried to grab her. "How could you? How could you, Macy? He was our son!" She was like a tropical storm as she flew through the room destructively, trying to get to Macy.

"It was an accident! Tima, listen to me!" Macy pleaded.

She backpedaled out of the room while shaking her head from side to side. "No, I'm done listening to you. I trusted you. You're a liar!" she shouted as mascara mixed with anguish and created trails of black tears down her cheeks.

Macy raced after her as he tried to explain. He had not expected her to return home. He had gotten loose with his lips and had spoken of Boomer's death too freely. Fatima ran until she made it to her car.

"Fatima!" Macy called out as she locked herself inside. She started the car and ignored him as he banged on the driver side window and pulled on the door handle. "Don't do this, Tima. Open the door, baby girl. Just hear me out!"

A distraught Fatima put the car in reverse and backed up slightly. She placed the car back in drive and pressed the gas all the way to the floor, aiming the car straight at Macy. He had pushed her to her breaking point. There was nothing that this man could say to fix what he had broken. He had deceived her and had manipulated her.

He saw me go through hell and all along it was because of what he did? she thought as uncontrollable tears flooded her. Fatima was in a state of shock as she tried to wrap her brain around the truth. She just didn't understand. After years of her holding Macy down and playing the back so that he could shine, how could he do this to her? Fatima had been a good wife to him, a loyal wife to him. She wasn't above doing dirt, but she had limits. Macy was never a target, and he would have never fallen into her crosshairs.

"How could you do this to us? How could you!" she shouted as she drew closer to him with her car, going full speed. Macy put his hands up in front of him, signaling for her to brake, but she never let up on the accelerator.

"Yo, she's not stopping, Macy! Get out of the way!" Edris yelled as he watched the domestic dispute unfold and escalate to a violent level. He knew Fatima well and had seen her temper flare once before, so he knew what she was capable of. This time even Edris had to admit that her outrage was warranted.

Macy stood his ground, not thinking that Fatima would actually hit him. When he noticed that she wasn't letting off the gas, he dodged the car just in the nick of time. All he saw were taillights as Fatima sped off of their property. "Fuck!" he shouted. "Put the word out that I'm looking for her."

Edris nodded his head and followed Macy as he stormed back into his home.

Fatima ripped through the city streets, crying nonstop. Her husband's betrayal was too much for her to handle alone. She needed help, but she had nowhere to go and no one to run to. Macy ran the entire city, so going to the police was not an option. She was stuck, and as the hours passed on the clock, she grew tired of roaming aimlessly. She found herself driving toward Santa Monica to see a man she hadn't spoken to in years.

Case had kept in close contact with Macy over the years, but his interactions with Fatima had been limited. They spoke briefly and cordially, but it was always too awkward for them to be too involved in each other's lives. Case had been the first man to show her love, and she had crushed him when she had chosen to be with Macy. Their friendship hadn't been the same since she had left him, but on this night, she needed him. She needed him more than she ever had before.

Fatima drove to the lavish beachside condo where he resided and parked her car on the street. The lights were on inside, and she knew that he was home, but she sat frozen as she thought of what she would say to him. What could she say? Karma had come full circle. She had betrayed Case to be with Macy, and ultimately Macy had hurt her. Macy had taken the one thing in her life that was irreplaceable.

She sat in the car for almost an hour, going back and forth in her mind as the cell phone rang repeatedly. Picking up the phone, she saw Macy's face flash before her eyes, and the sight of him made her sick to her stomach. She sent him to voice mail only for him to call right back. Disgusted, she powered off her phone. What could he possibly say to her? No words could take back his actions. What he had done was unforgivable.

Fatima gathered herself and pulled down her visor to fix her face, but when she saw her own reflection, she knew that she was too broken. There was no hiding her torment. No amount of makeup could conceal her hurt. Her eyes were red and swollen. The color of her skin was pale and had a green tint to it. She would have to face Case the way she was or not face him at all.

Fatima exited her car and walked up the walkway that led to his condo. She climbed the stairs that led to his front entrance and nervously rang the bell. She heard the chime sound on the inside, and she turned quickly on her heels, suddenly changing her mind. *Why did I come here?* she asked herself. *He can't save me now. I chose Macy.*

She heard the door open, but she didn't look back until he called her name. "Fatima?"

She froze but refused to face him.

"Tima, is everything all right?" he asked. Case's deep voice offered security to her in her vulnerable state. She was in need of protection, of comfort, and Case was the only person who she could think to turn to.

Case put his hand on his waistline, clicking his .45 off of safety, and turned on his porch light to make sure that Macy's goons weren't lurking in the shadows of the foliage that covered the front of his house. Fatima being at his home was too much of a coincidence for Case. He stepped out, ready to shoot anything moving as his neck swiveled from left to right. He was surprised to see that she was alone. He had thought she was sent as a decoy to distract him, but as he looked around cautiously, nothing seemed out of place.

"Are you by yourself?" he asked.

She nodded her head as she turned to face him.

"Why did you come here, Fatima?" he asked. It had been too long for this to be a coincidence. Any other day she barely gave him the time of day. Although her attraction to him had never dissipated, her respect for her husband always overrode anything she felt toward Case. For her to be on his doorstep in the middle of the night was a surprise to Case, and frankly, it was suspect.

As she stepped toward him, the light shone directly on her face, and he saw how distressed she appeared.

She lowered her head and ran into his arms as he hesitantly welcomed her into an unsure embrace.

"He killed him, Case," she sobbed as she cried into his chest. Her words came out mumbled, and Case held her, despite the fact that he had no idea what had gone on.

For the first time in fifteen years, he wrapped his arms around her intimately. She was sobbing so hard that she couldn't speak as she poured her soul into Case.

"What are you doing here, Tima? Macy know where you at?" he asked, his voice low as he loomed over her, resting his chin on top of her head.

"I . . . I have to talk to you," Fatima whispered as she pulled away from him. "It's important."

"Go home, Tima. Look at you. You're a mess. I don't know what happened between you and Macy, but you shouldn't be here," he replied. He had been very careful not to cross any lines or rekindle any old flames with her over the years. Their interactions were always so rehearsed, strategic, as if they were afraid to speak openly to one another. Now here they were, past lovers standing under a full moon as the Pacific Ocean left the scent of salt in the air.

"Please . . . I can't go back there. I just need to tell you something. Can we please go inside?" she asked as she pulled at his hand desperately, like a little girl pleading for help.

Case shook his head and put his arm around her shoulders as he led her into his home. He locked the door and pulled back his window drapes once more, his paranoia working overtime.

"It's just me. Macy has no idea where I am," she whispered as she wiped her red eyes. As she stared at Case, she couldn't contain her emotions. The features of his face were so familiar to her. It tugged at her heart as she stared at him carefully, studying every inch of him. Her eyes watered over and she shook her head. "All of this is my fault. I should have never left you to be with him," she whispered.

"Calm down, Fatima. Have a seat and tell me why you've come all the way here," he said soothingly as he pulled out a chair and motioned for her to sit.

She gripped his forearms for support because her legs threatened to give out at any moment. She looked around at Case's home and realized that it was her first time ever stepping foot inside.

"You've done really well for yourself." She sniffled, beating around the bush and avoiding the real reason why she was there. "You really did take over L.A., huh?" she asked in disbelief, remembering that he had always said he would when they were younger.

"Your husband isn't the only one getting money," Case replied smugly as he leaned back in his chair.

"He killed him, Case. He killed Boomer," Fatima choked out as she put her head in her hands as her tears leaked through her fingers.

Case frowned doubtfully. He had known Macy for a long time, and while he didn't doubt his gangster, he knew that he would never shoot his own son. "He loved Boomer, Fatima. I'm sorry about Boomer's death, but you can't put that on Macy. Boomer was troubled. It was the drugs. Macy wouldn't do that. Nothing in the world would make him kill his own son."

"It wasn't his son," she said. Her voice was so low that it was barely audible.

"What did you say?" Case asked.

"Boomer wasn't Macy's son," she repeated while still crying.

Case calculated the years in his head, and his heart dropped instantly as he put the pieces of the puzzle together. He knew that Fatima hadn't been with another man in years—eighteen years, to be exact—and he felt an ache in his chest that made it hard for him to breathe.

"He was yours, Case. Boomer was your son," Fatima admitted. She had told herself that she would never tell him, but now she felt as if he was the only person she could go to.

"What?" Case said, his anger surfacing.

Fatima lowered her head, too ashamed to face him.

"Don't look at the fucking floor, Fatima! Look at me. You can't just come up in here and drop a bomb like that! It's been eighteen years!" Case shouted. "And you're just now telling me I had a son?"

"I'm sorry!" she screamed in defense.

"You're sorry?" he shouted. His loud voice only made her cry harder, and he caught himself to avoid making things worse. He stood from his seat and paced the floor as he tried to process what she was telling him. His rationale went out the door as his emotions got the best of him. "He was my son?" he asked.

She nodded.

"How could you keep this from me?" he asked as his voice cracked. He cleared his throat to regain composure, and his eyes burned into hers, displaying his rage, revealing his uncertainty. He didn't know how to feel. He felt a combination of emotions, but sadness prevailed over them all. He had known Boomer, but not in the way that a man was supposed to know his son. They had never gotten a chance to bond or to even know one another. Case had never had a reason to become a better man. He lived for himself and took risk on top of risk because he wasn't afraid to die. He hadn't known that he would be leaving his firstborn son behind.

"I just wanted a better life for Boomer. You were in the streets, Case, living the fast life. You weren't ready to settle down, and you definitely were not fit to be a family man. I wanted to protect my son."

"And you call this protecting him?" Case shouted.

"I didn't mean for this to happen!" she defended. "When Macy and I started messing around, he was saying and doing all of the right things. He had plans, Case. He was going to school and getting out of the game. He was focused on me, whereas you were focused on many. You didn't think I knew about all of those other bitches?" She paused as she looked at Case knowingly. "I knew, Case, and I didn't want to be just another chick you were dropping off at the clinic!"

"You didn't even give me a chance, Fatima! You didn't tell me! You just took my son away and let the next nigga raise him! Does he know?" Case asked.

Fatima shrugged her shoulders, feeling overwhelmed.

"Don't tell me you don't know, bitch," Case said angrily. "Does he know that Boomer was my seed?" he asked sternly.

Fatima was keeled over in her chair crying her heart out and Case immediately felt bad. He knew that she was going through a lot, and he tamed his animosity before speaking again.

"I'm sorry, ma," he said as he knelt before her. "But you've got to tell me something. This is fucking me up. You have to help me understand why you would do this to me."

"I just wanted the best for my baby," she whispered.

"That could have been me, Tima," he replied. "I could have given you and Boomer the world. I was young and stupid back then, but a family would have helped me grow up. I would have changed for the two of you."

"I'm sorry," she whispered. She could see it in his eyes that he was struggling with her revelation.

"Did Macy know that Boomer wasn't his?" he asked again.

"I think he felt that Boomer wasn't his son, but he never spoke on it. Not once did he question me or speak his doubt aloud. He just took what I told him as truth, but I could see the skepticism in his eyes," Fatima replied.

Although Case didn't have a relationship with Boomer, he felt responsible to find the person responsible for the murder.

"What makes you think Macy killed him?" Case inquired.

"I heard him! He admitted it. The cocky bastard spoke the words out of his mouth! I heard him with my own ears," she said, disgusted. Her skin crawled as she thought of all the times she had made love to Macy after he had annihilated her flesh and blood. She had been bedding the enemy. "How could he even look me in the face after what he did?" All of her questions were rhetorical because she knew that no one could answer them except Macy.

Case gritted his teeth as he thought of his only son being betrayed by the man he thought of as a father. Jealousy filled him as he thought of all the milestones and memories that he had missed. Now it was too late to get those things back.

Macy's actions instantly changed Case's agenda. What was supposed to be a simple ransom kidnapping would be elevated to a murder. Case had a taste for revenge. He savored the flavor of vengeance on his tongue as he thought of ending Macy's life. He would order Macy a slow death, and he knew that Aries had some tricks up her sleeve that would bring the strongest of men to their knees. Taking his woman he had tolerated because he knew that Fatima had willingly walked away from him. He had partially blamed himself for losing her because he knew the game. He had lost his bitch because he had left a void within her that Macy was able to fill. Losing Fatima was partially on Case, but by fucking with his money and now murdering his seed, Macy had crossed the line.

"Come here," he said.

In need of guidance and a shoulder to cry on, she rushed to him as he held her tightly. The scent of her perfume tickled his nose, and as they embraced, he massaged her back gently.

"I'm so sorry, Case," she said.

"It's a'ight, ma," he replied. "I'ma take care of it."

"How?" Fatima cried helplessly.

"However you want me to," Case replied.

He pulled away from her and walked over to his liquor cabinet. He removed a bottle of cognac and poured himself a stiff drink. He didn't usually like to cloud his mind, but he needed the burden that Fatima had just given him to be temporarily lifted from his heart. He downed the drink in one gulp and then poured another one.

Fatima walked beside him and reached for her own glass. She lifted it up, and without a word he poured her a drink too. She sipped it slowly and enjoyed the burn as the smooth liquid fire heated her entire body.

She grabbed the entire bottle in one hand and carried her glass in another as she walked through Case's living room. Case watched the sway of her hips and admired the way that she commanded her environment, kicking off her Louboutins as if she were the lady of the house. She sat down on his plush sectional and pulled her feet up underneath her bottom, making herself comfortable as she sipped the strong drink somberly.

Fatima didn't indulge in alcohol often. She was a social drinker and usually never touched the grown-man drinks. The cognac hit her quickly, making her body warm instantly as she nursed her drink and soul simultaneously.

He watched her for a moment, taking her in. She had matured, but so much about her was exactly as he remembered it. Fatima was still a bad bitch and the most striking woman that Case had ever encountered. He had sampled a generous share of women in his day, and none of them held a candle to Fatima.

He silently wondered what it would have been like if he had never sent her home with Macy all those years ago. He hadn't known that his best friend would steal his girl and ultimately marry her. Case had lost a good thing when he had lost Fatima, and as he realized that she had given birth to his child, he suddenly wished that he could turn back the hands of time.

Fatima indulged in her drink silently, lost in her thoughts of sadness. She didn't even realize that Macy was standing over her until she heard him speak.

"Don't drink too much of that. It'll sneak up on you," he schooled as he sat across from her.

"It doesn't matter. Tonight I'm trying to get fucked up. I don't want to feel anything. . . . I just want to sit here and throw a pity party. I want to drink my drink and sit here until it doesn't hurt anymore," she admitted without shame.

She shook her head as Macy's face entered her mind. "He sat there for fucking weeks, watching me deteriorate. He heard me crying every night. He slept in my bed knowing that all along he had killed my son. Bastard." She finished her drink and then poured herself another as she continued to vent.

"How can he do something like that? After all of these years? I've stood by him, playing the back and being the supportive woman that he needed. I was there when he was just another dope boy. I helped him study night after night when he was in college. I even wrote some of his papers! I'm the one who went door to door, convincing people to vote for a black mayor. I smiled for the cameras and hosted the events. How could he kill Boomer? My son? I know the dirt he's done in order to get where he is, but I never thought that he was capable of hurting me . . . or hurting our son."

As soon as the words left her mouth, she immediately wished she could take them back. "I'm sorry, Case. I know he's your son. It's just . . . I'm . . . I'm so used to . . ."

"You don't have to explain, Fatima. I know what you meant," he replied.

"He can't get away with this. He has the entire police department in his pocket. My son will never get the justice he deserves," she cried.

"What's justice? Nothing is going to bring Boomer back," Case answered. He already knew what he was going to make happen. Macy would be sleeping with the fishes in due time, but he said all the right things in order to ease Fatima's suffering.

The drinks were starting to get to Fatima, which only intensified the anguish she was going through. It hurt so badly that all she could think of was revenge. She wanted Macy to lose something. Boomer had lost his life; it was only fair that Macy did too. "I want him dead," she whispered.

Case left his seat so that he could sit next to Fatima. He put his arm around the back of the couch and faced her. "You can't say things that you don't mean, Tima. A mu'fucka like me ain't afraid to make that happen, but you can't play with stuff like that. You don't even speak on that unless you ready to put on your little black dress and your widow's veil," he whispered in her ear.

Her breathing intensified as the feeling of his lips on her ear caused shivers to travel down her spine.

"I know that, Case, and I'm not just talking," she replied, her voice sultry and deep. "The man killed my son, my only baby. I'm serious. I want Macy dead."

"You know what you're asking for, right?" he asked. "Once that order is put in, there ain't no taking it back. Won't be no more going home to your husband. You say that's what you want, but you're in your feelings right now. It's not a game."

"I know what I want," she shot back.

Case knew that the liquor gave her the courage to express her true feelings aloud, and he was more than happy to oblige her.

"You forget this conversation ever happened. I'll take care of it," he whispered.

"You would do that for me? After all that I've done to you?" she asked in astonishment.

Case turned her face toward his and when he spoke, they were so close that their lips touched. "I would do that for my son," he said strongly.

A tear of regret fell down her face as she remembered why she used to love him. He had been her protector when she was not woman enough to stand up for herself. Yes, they had been young when they were together, but it was far from puppy love. She had just been greedy and had fallen for something forbidden. Karma had come full circle, and the very man she had loved wholeheartedly had hurt her to her core.

Case wiped the tear from her face and pulled her to him as he devoured her lips. She didn't hesitate as she opened her mouth and welcomed his tongue inside. The spark that they both felt told them that things had never truly ended between them. It felt right, it felt safe for her, but to Case it felt like the sweetest revenge. Macy had pulled his bitch on a drunken night, and now Case had turned right around and snatched her back under the same circumstances. As he removed her clothes, he couldn't help but smirk. This would undoubtedly be the most satisfying nut he ever busted.

Case's touch made goose bumps form on her skin. She would have been nervous, but the liquor calmed her tremendously, lowering her inhibitions. She had been feeling so downtrodden and depressed that the sensations Case were bringing her were welcomed. She spread her legs as he slipped his hand between her thighs, creeping up her dress and sliding her panties to the side with expertise. He was so skilled and smooth that before she could even protest, he was fingering her clit, making her mouth fall open in pure bliss. Blood flowed to her lower regions, making her southern lips swell and drool in anticipation.

"You want me to stop?" he asked, already knowing that she would say no.

She shook her head and closed her eyes as she worked her hips, grinding on his fingers. Seeing the look on her face was the sweetest revenge to Case. Having her here, playing in her pussy and hearing her moan as a result of his doing, made his dick hard.

Bitch-ass nigga never knew what to do with this pussy, he thought as he laid her down and positioned himself between her legs. He loosened his belt and pulled his Italian-threaded slacks down. He didn't even bother to take them off as he freed his hard-on from the confinements. History was about to repeat itself, and he was about to plant so many seeds in Fatima that she wouldn't have a choice but to bend to his will, mentally and physically.

He entered her and immediately tensed his body when he felt how tightly her womanhood hugged him. He still fit inside of her perfectly. The fit was so snug that it felt as if he would bust prematurely. She had him feeling like a teenage boy who was getting his first taste; her love was so good. He quickly composed himself and found his rhythm as she whispered his name repeatedly in his ear.

"Case . . . ooh, Case, I missed this dick," she crooned, seducing him with a sweet melody that fed his ego. He worked her middle as she grabbed his firm backside, pulling him into her wetness as she squeezed it.

He was so deep inside of her that he could hear her gush as he hit her G-spot. He felt her squirting over his shaft while he stroked her aggressively yet gently.

His pace sped up as he felt the head of his penis swell, and every stroke made his toes curl as his tool became extra sensitive. "Shit, ma," he complimented. Case could normally go for hours, but with Fatima he couldn't control himself.

He hit her hard, grinding and digging her out as deeply as he could, until he finally came. He made no effort to pull out. In fact, he pumped his semen inside of her with a smirk on his face as he thought of how he was disrespecting Macy. In fact, he made sure that he released every little bit of semen into her until he had nothing left.

Macy sat back and leaned his head back as he reveled in the euphoria. Fatima breathed heavily as she lay there wondering what life may have been like if she had never left Case. She wasn't ready for this to end. Having Case inside of her made her feel closer to her son. He was Boomer's father, and being with him again was like applying glue to her broken heart. Case was filling the sudden void that had entered her life.

He went to stand, but she grabbed his hand and pulled him back down onto the couch. It may have seemed desperate, but Fatima knew that as long as he was making her feel good, she wouldn't feel anything else. She mounted him and pulled her dress off of her shoulders, exposing her D-cups and lace bra. His hands covered her caramel mounds, and within seconds, his erection had returned. She slid down on top of him and rode him slowly as she closed her eyes.

Bedding Fatima after years of her being absent in his life boosted Case's ego. She had strayed and had betrayed him by marrying his best friend, but like a loyal dog, she had come back home. Now it was time for Macy to get a dose of his own medicine.

Case's beef with Macy had been unsettled for too long. Over the years, the two had continued to do business and money had healed old wounds, but now Macy thought he was too legit to deal with Case. On top of that, he had killed his son, which only fueled an already out-of-control fire.

Case looked at Fatima as she moved her magnificent body up and down on his shaft. He could tell she was irrational and making a decision that she would later regret, but he didn't care. The fact that she had found her way back into his bed worked to his advantage, and once Case put word into Aries, it was only a matter of time before Macy was no longer an issue. Case was about to make an example out of Macy once and for all.

Chapter Ten

"Hi, you've reached Fatima Sigel. I'm unavailable to take your call—"

Macy slammed his executive phone down as he heard his wife's voice mail pick up once again. He had been trying to reach her all night to no avail. Frustrated and fearing the unknown, Macy pinched the bridge of his nose as he tried to calm himself. He knew that she had not gone to the police because no one had come knocking on his door asking questions.

Macy wondered where she could be. He had traced all of her credit card transactions, trying to see if she had checked into a hotel, but he had come to a dead end. Fatima didn't want to be found, and he would have to respect that until she chose to reach out to him.

From the look on her face, Macy realized that things would never be the same between them. There was no explanation that he could give that would erase the monstrous image that she had of him now. The fact that he had not intended to harm Boomer didn't matter. The truth was obsolete at this point. She had already rendered him guilty, and Macy didn't know what that meant for him. Fatima was a woman scorned, and Macy had no idea how to rectify the problem.

Had she been anyone else, he could have handled it easily. One phone call could make the situation disappear; but she was his wife, and despite what they were going through, he loved her. He cherished her and only wanted to protect her, which was why he hadn't come out and told her the truth from the beginning.

His phone rang nonstop as his secretary tried to contact him. He had already missed his entire morning's schedule. Macy couldn't even run his own household. How the hell did anyone expect him to run the city? He couldn't focus on his professional life when his personal one was in such disarray. The information that Fatima had on him was sensitive, and she needed to know that their family skeletons needed to be kept in the closet. It was imperative that she cooperate. Macy knew that the longer she stayed away, the worse it would be for him in the end. He just needed her to hear him out.

Distracted, he headed out for his office. The expectations that were placed on his shoulders normally would not be an issue, but with Fatima missing and his life in shambles, work was the last thing on his mind. He grabbed his leather briefcase and tightened his tie before he walked outside and entered the town car that was waiting in front of his home.

"City Hall, and don't take the expressway. I don't want to get caught up in traffic," he called out.

Macy closed his eyes and rested his head on the back of the leather seat as the car pulled away from his home. He was abruptly startled when he heard a loud pop as one of the tires burst and the car slowed to a stop.

"What's going on?" he asked the driver.

"I don't know. Sounds like I ran over something sharp."

The driver got out of the car, and Macy did as well, and when he looked at one of the rear tires, he saw that it was completely shredded to pieces. Exasperated, he sighed as he turned to the driver. "How long is it going to take to fix this?" he asked.

"Not long at all. There should be a spare in the trunk. I know you're not dressed for this, but could you give me a hand?" the driver asked.

Macy walked to the rear of the car as the driver popped the trunk, and when he saw the body of Frank, his normal driver, lying bloody inside, his eyes bugged in horror. He was completely taken off guard, and as he turned around, he stared down the barrel of a .357 handgun.

Aries pulled off her hat and long, flowing hair spilled out as she shook it loose while she lightly gripped the trigger.

"Get in," she said.

Macy was taken aback that he was being held at gunpoint by a woman—a beautiful woman, at that. He didn't know who she was and made the mistake of trying to talk her down.

"Look. I don't know who sent you or what you want, but—"

Aries shot the gun, sending a bullet flying so close to his face that he felt the wind as it blew by his cheek, slightly grazing him.

"Shit! Whoa! Wait a minute," Macy yelled as he put his hands up defensively, fearing that her next shot would go through his skull.

"I'm a very impatient woman. Next time I won't miss. Get in the trunk," she said forcefully.

She knew that the deserted road wouldn't stay empty for long. She was lucky to even get the opportunity to get to Macy. She had been on him for weeks and could not find a way to get at him. He stayed with security and bodyguards. She also noticed how he always kept a pistol on his hip. The way that he walked with his hands near his waistline told her that he stayed strapped. Aries knew that if she blew this attempt at snatching him, another opportunity would be near impossible. It was now or never, and she had the upper hand at the moment because she was the one holding the gun. She had caught him slipping.

Macy pushed the dead body to the back of the trunk and then climbed in. He barely had his entire body inside before she closed the trunk on him, immersing him in nothing but darkness. Anger filled him more than actual fear. "Fuck!" he yelled as he hit the trunk above him with a flat hand.

He didn't know who was behind this, but his anger made the hood in him come out as his mind went through the possibilities. He had rubbed a lot of people the wrong way. From the streets to the political world, he knew a dozen niggas who had beefs to pick with him, but he had never expected anyone to go this far. He thought that his reputation alone and his status would keep him safe and protected. It was clear to him now that his expensive suits and his celebrity didn't make him off-limits. He was still a target, and he had a feeling that someone was about to make some steep demands—demands that he was afraid he wouldn't be able to meet.

Macy fumbled in the trunk as the smell of the body turned his stomach. He could feel his clothes become saturated as he lay in a pool of the dead man's blood. *Whoever is behind this ain't fucking around. And they sent a bitch after me,* he thought.

He reached for his cell phone and pulled it out. He quickly dialed Edris' number. Hope filled him as he kicked at the taillights from the inside of the car. If he could just get an idea of where he was being taken, he knew that his right hand would come looking for him. He kicked with all of his might, until finally the taillight popped out.

He looked at his screen and saw that his phone was calling Edris; however, the phone's signal dropped before he could get through.

"No . . . no . . . damn it!" he shouted as he tried to redial the number only to receive the same results. He had no cell reception from the trunk and couldn't get a call to go through.

He pushed the taillight that was closest to his head until it too popped out. He hoped that the police would spot the vehicle and pull the girl over. He stuck his hand out of the back of the car, hoping to attract attention. He craned his neck awkwardly until he could see out of the back and then waved his hand back and forth at the car that had just gotten behind them.

HONK! HONK!

Macy's heart sped up when he heard the car honking. *HONK!*

He felt the car slow down as the pace of his heart sped up. Macy knew that this would be his only chance to get out of the situation. He knew the game; it wasn't too long ago that he was stuffing niggas in trunks himself, and he knew that if he didn't make it out of that trunk, then he was as good as dead.

The car came to an abrupt stop on the side of the road, and Macy began beating on the top of the trunk.

"Hey! Hey! I'm in here! Let me out! Help me!" he shouted at the top of his lungs.

"Fuck is you doing?" he heard the woman shout as she got out of the car and approached the driver who had stopped behind her. He watched as the two exchanged words, but he couldn't hear what was being said over the hum of the engine. When Macy saw the young man walk up to the trunk, he got louder.

He heard the trunk release pop, and he pushed up on the metal, causing sunlight to spill inside. As he began to sit up, he was hit with a pistol across his face, knock-ing him out cold. What he had thought was help was really Aries' accomplice.

"You got the nigga in the trunk drawing crazy atten-tion to the whip. He's out cold now, and he shouldn't be waking up anytime soon. We'll have enough time to get him to the spot without any trouble," the young goon stated.

Aries nodded her head and was glad that she had decided to bring backup. She hadn't wanted to under-estimate Macy, and her instincts had proved correct. There was no telling who would have seen the taillights if Case's young gunner, Harlo, had not been following them.

Case had hooked her up with two reckless stick-up kids who weren't afraid to put in work. The other boy was waiting at a rental property across town. It was where they would hold Macy and eventually take his life.

Aries didn't know what had caused Case to change his mind and escalate the situation from kidnapping to murder, but it wasn't her place to ask questions. As she closed the trunk back down on Macy, she was glad that he was unconscious. His actions would have gotten more innocent people involved, and although she did not want to, she would not hesitate to pop anyone who tried to play hero and get in the way. Aries was there to do a job, and she had more at stake than anyone involved. Case was threatening her family and when it was all said and done, they meant more to her than Macy ever would. She would eliminate him in order to look out for her own on any given day. Anyone else who got hurt in the process would be unfortunate, but it was all a part of the game.

***

Aries and Harlo dragged Macy into the house where their third accomplice, Jordan, was waiting impatiently. The impatient and worried look on his face told Aries that he was scared. The young boys were amateurs, and as she pulled Macy inside, she saw the look of recognition on the boy's face.

"Fuck! That's who the vic is?" Jordan asked as he put both hands on the sides of his head. "Do you know who the fuck that is? That's Macy Sigel. The police are going to be all over this shit when they find out this nigga is missing!"

"Shut the fuck up, you bitch-ass nigga. I wouldn't give a fuck if this was the mu'fuckin' president. Come help me move this nigga," Harlo shot as he struggled to lift Macy's limp body into a wooden chair.

Jordan shook his head and replied, "I don't want shit to do with this, fam. Didn't nobody say nothing about him being the mayor."

Aries stood back and watched the interaction between the two as she stood with her hands on her hips. She shook her head in frustration. She was so used to working with seasoned killers. Aries hadn't feared anyone in so long that she forgot how it felt to be new to the game. She could sense the trepidation in Jordan.

"Look, you're already involved. It's too late for any of us to back out now. You know too much," Aries stated. Her words came out nicely, but the curt smile on her face delivered the threat, causing goose bumps to form on the young kid's arms. "Now, take his ass in the basement and tie him up," she instructed.

"It's time to wake up," Aries stated as she sat in a chair directly across from Macy. She slapped his face repeatedly to arouse him from his forced slumber.

Macy slowly came to, and when he opened his eyes, he bucked violently, lunging for Aries. She didn't flinch and put her face inches away from his, taunting him. She could tell that he was used to power, and the fact that she had caught him slipping was an insult to him. Macy just didn't know who Aries was. If he did, he would know that he was one of many powerful men to get tangled in her deadly web.

"I'm going to have to break you in, I see," she said, noticing his obvious defiance. "You don't fear me yet, but you should," Aries said. She retrieved a silencer from the bag of guns that Case had provided her with and slowly screwed it onto the tip of her pistol. "I'm going to show you that I'm not playing games. You don't want to fuck with me," she threatened. She placed the tip of the gun on his left hand and blew a hole clear through it.

"Aghh!" Macy shouted in excruciating pain as his hand exploded with heat and blood spilled all over the floor. She looked at him closely as a light sweat formed on his brow.

The two goons were silent as they watched in amazement like spectators as she put her game down like it was a sport. Harlo respected it and found it extremely sexy, but Jordan, on the other hand, feared Aries because he knew that he had gotten in over his head.

"Macy Sigel, you're going to tell me what I want to know, or we can do this all day," she threatened.

Macy couldn't believe how callous the woman before him was. Blood dripped from his hand as he bit down on his inner jaw to keep from crying out in pain.

The two of them locked eyes—a war of the worlds, of egos, of reputations. Aries had done her homework, and she knew that Macy was a wolf in sheep's clothing. The fancy suits didn't fool her. He was just like her.

They were from the same world, and she knew what he was capable of. The shoe could have easily been on the other foot under different circumstances. Macy's power knew no limits on the streets or with the law, and Aries knew that she would have to be careful with this job. As long as she kept the upper hand, things would go smoothly.

"Where's the money?" Aries asked.

"Money?" he replied as he scoffed in exasperation. He shook his head from side to side. "That's what this is all about. I have plenty money, sweetheart. I run this city. I'm a very wealthy man. This can be solved before this gets out of hand. Why don't you untie me and let's handle this in a more civilized way." Macy's voice was calm and convincing, despite the blinding pain that shot through his hand and arm.

Had Aries been anyone else, the words that Macy spoke would have been appealing, but he only angered her. "Don't patronize me, Mr. Mayor," she said as she jammed the tip of her gun into the hole in his hand, causing his wound to bleed profusely.

He bit down into his lip as his nostrils flared. "Aghh!" he shouted.

"You can't get in my head, but I know a million and one ways to get inside of yours," Aries said as she whispered in his ear.

"Why are you doing this?" he asked. "I told you I can get you some paper. Who are you working for?" Macy asked, breathing hard.

Aries smirked as she pulled up a chair and sat across from Macy. She crossed her legs and said, "Men like you are so funny. Look at you. You're tied to a chair, bleeding, sitting in front of someone who can end your life at any minute, and the first thing you want to know is who sent me? You've crossed that many people that you don't even know who your enemies are." She pulled out her cell phone and placed a call.

Case answered on the first ring. He had been waiting anxiously to hear from her, but before he could say too much over the phone, she spoke.

"I've got him," she stated and then hung up.

Macy was silent, but he listened closely as she spoke. He knew that in his situation, talking would get him dead fast. The less information he gave up, the more time he bought himself.

Aries was more gangster than most men he knew. It was obvious that this wasn't her first rodeo. The fact that she was so comfortable pulling a trigger told Macy that he was in trouble. Under any other circumstance he would have recruited her to work for him, because he knew that it was wise to keep people like her close to avoid being a target of hers later.

He racked his brain trying to figure out who was behind this little fiasco, but he came up with nothing. Macy ran Aries' face through his mental Rolodex, desperate to place her face with a name, but he knew that he didn't know her. Not many people would forget a face like hers.

Macy didn't give a damn what she did. He realized that things were beyond repair now. There was no way that he would make it out of this situation alive. He wasn't for the head games. He was too stubborn to allow Aries to manipulate him into telling her anything. If she thought that he was going to make it easy on her, she was mistaken.

Aries left the basement and hours passed as day turned to night. He could no longer feel his arm. Time betrayed him as every minute felt like torture. He heard the basement door open and watched as Aries descended the stairs. A tall figure came down behind her, and when Macy laid eyes on Case, he gritted his teeth in anger. As soon as he saw Case's face, everything became so clear. He should have known that there was only one man in the city who had enough gumption to go after the mayor. Case didn't live by anyone's rules except his own, and he didn't fear the repercussions that came along with snatching Macy. If the kidnapping got out, then every badge in the city would be looking for him, but Case didn't care. He didn't fear Macy or the law.

"Long time no see," Case stated calmly as he sat down in the chair across from Macy and puffed the Cuban cigar that he held in his hand.

Everything made sense to Macy now, and reality hit him like a ton of bricks. Case had always held animosity toward Macy. He should have known that eventually things would go sour between them. They had made good money together back in the day, but their mutual love for the same woman had torn their business relationship apart. As Macy stared at Case with malice, the tension could be felt throughout the room.

"I should have known," Macy stated. "It's just like you to have a bitch do your dirty work for you."

Case smugly blew cigar smoke in Macy's face before putting it out directly on Macy's cheek.

"Hmmm! Hmmm!" Macy screamed through clenched jaws as the cigar seared his skin.

"I think you have something that belongs to me," Case said.

Macy chuckled as he shook his head from side to side. "Still the same old Case. You've always been a lazy-ass nigga looking for a handout. I don't owe you shit."

"No?" Case asked. He reached into the pocket of his suit jacket and removed a tiny black book. Inside were

handwritten records, a ledger that could put Macy behind bars if it ever got into the wrong hands. Any time
a money transaction had gone down between the old
friends, Case had kept track. "You sitting up high on
that mayor's throne, but you forgot who helped you
get there. Before this city even knew your name I was
backing you. You built your entire campaign off of dirty
money and then you turned your back on me . . . on the
streets that raised you."

"I grew up; I didn't forget shit. The community that
I came up in is the same one that I'm putting state dollars back into," Macy defended.

"Nah, I'm not talking about no programs, Macy. I'm
talking about looking out for the li'l niggas you had
posted on the block hustling up your campaign dollars.
I'm talking about all of the endorsements, all of the
cash payments I put up to have other public officials
stand behind you. You didn't have shit but a degree.
I put up so much money that I should have been your
running mate.

"You was supposed to keep the streets clear for me.
Pull the police off of my ass when things got hot. But
what do you do? You become the city's savior and
change your entire platform as soon as you're elected.
This save-the-streets bullshit you created is making me
lose money, and I don't take L's. You broke our agree-
ment, and now I've come to collect my paper." Case
dangled the ledger in front of Macy's face arrogantly.

"According to this, you owe me seven hundred and
twenty thousand dollars."

Macy frowned when he heard the amount. "Fuck
is wrong with you? You doing all of this for chump
change? All you had to do was come to me like a man
and we could have settled this."

Case scoffed at Macy's cockiness. "Nah, I don't want that bank money. I want what I gave to you. It's too easy for you to pull that mayor money out of an account. I want the same dirty money that you built your career off of, and you've got forty-eight hours to come up with it or Fatima is going to be a widow."

Case's demands made no sense to Macy, but he wasn't in a position to ask questions. He knew exactly what money Macy was talking about. All of the street money that Macy had stacked had been put up for a rainy day. Getting Case the type of money he wanted wouldn't be easy.

Irony mocked Macy because the money that he had killed Boomer over was the same money that Case was going to kill him over. Macy knew that there was no way to get Case the type of money that he wanted. After Boomer's fiasco, all Macy had were legitimate funds. In addition to having a nice-sized bank account, he had access to countless funds through the city's treasury. He could easily take a little bit from each of the city's expense accounts, but that wasn't what Case wanted. He wanted dirty money, and it was the one thing that Macy could not get. His block-hugging and illegal enterprise–running days were over. Macy had too much to lose to even allow the allure of the streets to call him back, but Case was forcing his hand. If he didn't come up with the money, Case was going to make good on his threat.

Case kept a stone face but smiled inside as he watched the wheels turning in Macy's head. He had known him long enough to notice the stress lines appear in his forehead. Their friendship had never truly been genuine, even from the beginning. It was more like a competition, and Macy had been winning for too long. Case had just turned the tables and tipped the odds in his favor.

"I want my money," Case stated as he pulled out a burnout cell phone that he had purchased from a random store. "I think you need to make a couple phone calls. You keep this shit out of the press. If it gets out, you're dead."

He nodded at Harlo. "Untie one of the nigga hands," Case instructed.

He then looked at Macy seriously. "You try anything cute and I'm going to blow your muthafuckin' brains out," he said.

Macy reluctantly snatched the phone and put in a call to Big E. Macy nervously counted the rings as he thought that the voice mail was going to pick up. Finally he heard his right-hand man answer the line.

"Hello?"

"Edris, it's me," Macy stated.

"Where you been, fam? Shit's been on the news about you playing hooky all day. I've been blowing you up—"

"Listen, E, and listen close. It's important," Macy stated, cutting his man off. "I need you to find that paper that Boomer lost. It's important."

"Is everything a'ight, fam? You don't sound too good," Edris stated suspiciously.

"I'm in a sticky situation, fam. I'm not going to lie to you. I need that dough. If you don't come through on that, things are going to go real bad for me. You understand?" Macy asked.

The line went silent as Edris interpreted Macy's words. "What's going on?" he asked, feeling that something wasn't right.

"I just need that, Big E. In forty-eight hours I need you to have that paper for me. I need seven hundred twenty thousand in two days. It can't come from the bank. I'm going to be tied up until you get that for me,"

Macy stated, hoping that Edris was catching the subtle clues that Macy was giving him. "Do not let the press get wind of anything negative, and find Tima. Let her know that I love her and that I never meant to hurt her, E."

"Sounds like you're giving me your last words to your wife," Edris stated, finally realizing what was happening. "You can tell her that yourself once I come up with this dough. I got you, fam."

"Call me back at this number when you get it together, and when you come to deliver it, don't come alone," Macy said.

Case snatched the phone and hung it up abruptly; then in one swift movement, he pulled a pistol and struck Macy across the face with it. His head snapped violently to the right as his lip busted on impact. Macy took the blow and slowly pulled his head upright as he calmly spit the blood from his mouth.

"I told you not to get cute," Case stated. He was showing Macy no mercy. "You've got two days to get me my money, and don't worry about your wife. I'll let Fatima know you love her," Case stated slyly. "I'll whisper it in her ear when I slide my dick up in her tonight."

Hearing those words set Macy off as he lunged for Case, injured and all. The chair toppled over, and Case laughed loudly and obnoxiously.

Case walked over to Macy and kicked him in the stomach then gathered himself, dusting the wrinkles out of his designer suit. He exhaled loudly as he turned to Aries.

"Don't let this nigga out of your sight. I want somebody on him at all times," Case stated. "I'll let you know when it's time to put in that work."

Aries had been sitting back watching the entire thing. "Once this is over, you and I are even. I won't owe you a damn thing. Are we clear?" she stated with authority.

Case stepped closer to Aries, completely attracted by her femininity and intrigued by her gangster all at the same time. "If you had the right man in your life, you wouldn't even be in this position right now," he said, throwing out bait to see where her head was.

She scoffed and raised an arched eyebrow. "Don't even. You'll just embarrass yourself," she advised. Aries hated Case, and under any other circumstances she would have loved to make him her target, but he had her between a rock and a hard place. She was indebted to him; therefore, he had the upper hand, and that fact was common knowledge between them.

He nodded his head, taking her rejection in stride, and then left the house. Case was fully confident that Aries could handle the job, and he walked away with no worries, knowing that soon enough Macy wouldn't even be a factor.

Chapter Eleven

Edris rolled down Rodeo Drive looking for a man the streets called Chicago Larry. Edris knew that his old associate controlled the strip and its whores. Although it was 2011, he somehow found a way to be a successful pimp. Anything that went down on the strip, Chicago knew about it or had something to do with it.

Edris scanned the block as he slowly cruised down the avenue. He hoped that he saw one of the candy-red Cadillacs that Chicago was known to drive. Chicago Larry had pimped hard throughout the city for years. Edris knew that the underworld of prostitution started and ended with him. Edris didn't know where to begin looking for the hooker who stole from Boomer, but he knew that finding Chicago was a good start.

Edris pulled into the diner that Chicago was known to post at. Edris slightly smiled when he saw the candy-red car parked toward the back. "Bingo," he whispered as he parked the car.

A sense of urgency overcame Edris as he maneuvered his rather big body out of the car. He knew that he was playing with borrowed time and his boss's life depended on if he could get the money back. Edris walked into the small diner, and it was empty except for a couple of waitresses who stood behind the long counter. Edris immediately spotted Chicago sitting at the back table with an Asian young lady.

Edris made his way toward him, and as he got closer
he noticed that the lady across from Chicago was giving him a manicure. Chicago was a very tall man with
a slim build. He had a neat Caesar haircut and wore an
Italian-cut suit, a far cry from the stereotypical pimp.
He looked more like a stockbroker than a seller of
women.

"Well, you don't say," Chicago smoothly said with his
light voice.

"It's been a long time," Edris said as he held out his
hand. Chicago stood up and locked hands with Edris as
he embraced him.

"Well, welcome to my office. Have a seat, big man. I
know you here to talk about something. I haven't seen
you on the strip since you used to run packs for Macy,"
Chicago said as he displayed his huge gap in his two
front teeth.

He looked down at the girl who was once doing his
nails and whispered. "Okay, baby, time for you to get
back out there," he said as he looked outside onto the
street. Just as quick as the words came out of Chicago's
mouth, the girl had hurried out to walk the track.

Chicago watched as his girl went out the door and
then focused his attention back on Edris. "What's on
your mind?" Chicago asked as he sat down.

Edris sat down across from him and wasted no time
telling him what was going on. "Look, a short while ago
someone got robbed by a hooker. That somebody who
got robbed happened to be Macy's son. You hear anything about that?" Edris asked as he looked deep into
Chicago's eyes, trying to read him.

"No, can't say that I have. That shit been all over the
news though. His son got killed in the hotel, right?"
Chicago asked, but he already knew the answer. It had
been on the local news nonstop ever since the body was
found.

"Yeah, unfortunately," Edris said as he dropped his head and shook it from side to side. Edris was also playing a role because he knew who was responsible for the killing.

Edris looked at Chicago once again and continued, "You see, some money came up missing and it needs to get found . . . and needs to get found soon," Edris said as his voice got more threatening with each word. The intensity in his eyes displayed his seriousness.

"Dig this. I don't know anything about no whore with stolen money. Shit, if I did, I sure wouldn't be on this here strip pimping. Believe that!" Chicago said as nervousness was evident in his voice.

Edris noticed that little sweat beads were forming on Chicago's nose and his voice was becoming shaky. This automatically threw up red flags with Edris. The fact that Chicago claimed he knew nothing about stolen money made Edris suspicious. Edris knew Chicago, and the fact was that he pimped and pimped hard. Edris was not going to believe that Chicago didn't know anything about the entire situation.

"Okay, playboy. If you hear anything, give me a call," Edris said as he reached into his inside pocket.

Chicago Larry tensed up as Edris' hand slipped into his coat, and his eyes grew big as golf balls. Edris slightly smirked and pulled out a business card. "Here is my card," Edris said as he dropped the card on the table and stood up. He shook Larry's sweaty hand and left the diner.

Edris knew that Chicago knew more than what he was telling him, but Edris was determined to find out what Chicago was hiding.

Just as Edris exited through the door, Chicago quickly reached into his jacket and pulled out the cell phone. He waited for a response as he nervously kept his eye on the door, hoping Edris would not return.

Chicago grabbed a napkin off the table to wipe the sweat from his face as someone answered the other end.

"Dig this. Pack up all our shit. We are leaving a little bit earlier than we planned. Bitch, I will be there in ten minutes. You betta be ready in five," Chicago said just before he hung up the phone and took a deep breath. He thought that he would have more time before he had to flee town. The hooker who stole the money from Boomer was his bottom girl, and he was the one who told her to rob her client. He didn't know it was Macy's son until everything came out in the news. His popularity in pimping actually worked against him in this case, and Edris knew exactly who to look for when something went down on the strip.

Chicago waited a good five minutes and then headed out the door. He was about to head home, get the money, and get out of Dodge. He knew what Macy was capable of and didn't want any part of his wrath.

Macy felt his leg numbing up and his stomach began to have shooting pains. He looked over at Jordan, who sat in the chair across the room watching television. Macy tried to maneuver himself in a more comfortable position as he grimaced and bit his bottom lip.

"Yo, let me use the bathroom. I got to piss," Macy said as he grabbed his crotch. Jordan looked at the door and then back at Macy before he hesitantly responded.

"I'm not supposed to let you move from that spot," Jordan said, almost as if he were pleading with Macy.

"What am I supposed to do, piss my pants? Come on. Let me just go take a leak. You can go with me," Macy said as he noticed that his words were convincing the naïve thug.

"Okay, but we have to make it quick," Jordan said as he hesitantly grabbed the keys off of the television stand.

Just as he stood up, Harlo came storming through the door. "You ain't going anywhere, fam. Chill out trying that slick shit. You can handle your business in this," Harlo said as he tossed Macy an empty soda bottle. Harlo had been listening from the other room and came to stop a potential bad situation.

Harlo grabbed Jordan by the arm and pulled him to the side. "What the fuck are you doing, man? You can't let this mu'fucka out of your sight. Don't let the tie fool you. That nigga is a cold-blooded killer. You are being too soft right now," Harlo whispered harshly as he squeezed his partner's arm tightly.

"I just was going to let him use the bathroom, that's it. Why you bugging?" Jordan said, not fully understanding the mistake that he was about to make.

"Look, just don't let that nigga out of your sight. I can't leave you alone with this nigga for five minutes before you do some dumb shit," Harlo said as he shook his head from side to side and unleashed Jordan's arm.

"All right. Damn," Jordan said as he sat back down in the chair and stared at the small television that sat on the stand. Harlo took a seat next to him and looked at his watch, wondering where Aries was.

Edris sat in the back of the parking lot and sank low in his seat. He had waited for Chicago Larry to exit so that he could follow him. Edris had a gut feeling that he would lead him to the money.

Edris had only been waiting in the parking lot for a few minutes, and just as he expected, Chicago came out looking nervous. Chicago didn't notice Edris' car parked in the back as he scanned the lot and then hurried to his Cadillac. Chicago started his car up, and so did Edris. Chicago smoothly slid out of the parking lot, unaware that he was being followed.

"What are you so damn nervous for?" Edris whispered to himself as he stayed two car lengths behind Chicago and tailed him.

Ten minutes later Chicago was pulling into the driveway of a single-family home. Edris parked three houses down and watched as Chicago hurried out of the car and flew into the house. Not even two minutes later, he was rushing back outside with two duffle bags in his hand and a whore following close behind.

"I knew it!" Edris said as he put the pedal to the floor, blocking Chicago's car in the driveway. Edris pulled out his gun and hopped out of the car. It all happened so quickly, Chicago never saw it coming. Before he knew it, Edris had a gun in his face.

"What's in the bag, mu'fucka?" Edris asked as he reached inside of the window and snatched the bag that rested on Chicago's lap. The whore screamed at the top of her lungs as she held up her hands.

"Shut your bitch up before I send two through her," Edris warned as he grew irritated with her yelling.

"Shut up, bitch!" Chicago said as he quickly glanced over at the girl. The girl almost instantly closed her mouth.

Edris peeked in the bag while still having the gun pointed at Chicago. Just as he expected, it was full of money.

"What do we have here?" Edris asked with a sinister smile.

"Man, I hit the lotto the other day," Chicago lied as he let out a nervous chuckle. Edris almost instantly struck him in the head with his gun, making Chicago's forehead split and bleed.

"Don't fucking play with me. Now, where is the rest of it?" Edris said, knowing that it didn't look anywhere close to a million dollars.

"Okay, okay. I put half of it at one of my bitches' houses," Chicago said.

He regretted staying in town and not splitting when he first got the money. His greed wouldn't let him miss the upcoming Friday and Saturday. Those two days were his most lucrative, and he didn't want to miss out on old some good old-fashioned trick money. *Damn*, he thought to himself as he shook his head from side to side in resentment.

Edris hopped into the back seat. He then put his gun to Chicago's ribs. "Let's go," Edris said as he pushed the nose of his gun deeper into Chicago, making him feel the steel.

Chicago looked into his rearview mirror and put the car in reverse. He drove onto his lawn to move around Edris' car and made his way to the spot where the rest of the money was stashed.

Aries knocked at Case's door wanting to get things settled. She tapped her feet impatiently against the pavement and waited for the door to open. Moments later, Case answered the door with his shirt off and a blunt hanging from his mouth.

"We need to talk," Aries said as she brushed past him and went to the middle of the floor. She was obviously frustrated and she was ready to end the fiasco that Case had her involved in.

Case took a long drag of his blunt and opened his arms. "What? No hello?" he asked sarcastically.

"Fuck you, Case," Aries said as she pulled off her oversized designer shades. "Listen, I don't know what type of sick game that you are playing, but it needs to stop. I got the nigga like you asked me to do. What else is it? I am not a muthafuckin' babysitter," Aries said, not liking the current situation.

"Just be calm. I need my money first and then you can off the nigga," Case said nonchalantly as he puffed his weed-filled cigar.

"I am not a kidnapper. I am a killer. You are going way out of bounds with this one, Case," Aries said as she placed her hands on her hips in frustration.

"First of all, you need to lower your fuckin' voice in my house," Case said as he put his cigar out in the ashtray and clenched his jaws so tightly that you could see his jawbone. Then he continued, "Secondly, I don't think you are in a position to be making any demands. You are going to do what the fuck I want you to do, remember that. How would your husband feel if he knew you . . . the real you? You can drop your accent and wear heels with fancy clothes all you want, but I know how you really are. You are hood just like me," Case said as he stared intensely at Aries.

Aries hated to admit it, but Case was right. She had no other options but to play by Case's rules. He was in a position to hurt her family, and she didn't want to jeopardize their wellbeing.

Aries thought about pulling the gun she had in her purse and letting off two in Case's head. He was clearly unstrapped, and she would end it all with that one kill.

"Don't think about it," Case said as if he were reading her mind. "If something happens to me, you better believe someone will be at your front door, killing your husband and son," Case said as he smiled and tried to lighten up the mood by offering Aries a drink.

"I'll pass," Aries said as her trigger finger itched. She knew that Case had her number, so the only thing she could do was play by his rules.

"I just need you to hold the nigga there until that money comes up, and then after that, you can off him. Be patient, baby girl," Case answered.

Case would never let Aries know, but he respected her gangster. He knew that her and her old squad were nothing to play with in their prime, and that was the main reason he once hired them.

Aries now had to sit back and play the waiting game. She stormed out and headed back to the house.

Chicago pulled into the small apartment complex that one of his whores lived in. "This is it right here. She lives on the third floor," Chicago said as he looked up at the building.

"Okay, let's go up," Edris said as he held the gun firmly to Chicago's rib.

Edris looked over the girl in the front seat. She was noticeably shaken up, and Edris didn't have time to worry about two people while they went up and got the money. "You get your ass in the trunk!" Edris said as he hopped out, grabbed the keys out of the ignition, and waved his gun toward the trunk.

The hooker and Chicago got out of the car, and Edris quickly grabbed the girl and pushed her to the back of the car while still keeping a close eye on Chicago. The girl began to cry as Edris popped the trunk. Chicago quickly encouraged her that everything would be all right.

"Just get in there, baby girl. We will be right out. I promise," Chicago said, not knowing if he was being truthful or not.

The whore gained up enough courage and hopped in the trunk. Edris immediately closed the door and pointed the gun at Chicago.

"Let's go, nigga! Don't try any funny shit either. I'm shooting first and asking questions last, just to let you know," Edris added for insurance.

Chicago, with his hands still in the air, responded. "She should be up there," he said as he looked up to the third floor where the light was on.

Edris walked behind Chicago and pressed the gun to his lower back. They headed up the stairs and reached the door. Slow music leaked from the apartment, so Edris immediately knew that somebody was in there. Edris' mind began to race as he thought about what he potentially was walking into.

What if this nigga got goons waiting on the inside, Edris thought as Chicago knocked on the door. Edris dismissed the small amount of fear in his heart and knew that he had to go all out for his boss. He had to get the rest of the money or Macy would die.

Moments later, a female voice sounded from the opposite side of the door. "Who is it?" she said in an irritated tone.

"It's me, bitch. Now, open the door!" Chicago yelled as he leaned into the door.

Seconds later the door opened and the sounds of smooth R&B came out of the apartment along with the smell of incense. A young black girl answered the door wearing nothing but an undersized silk robe. She held the robe closed with her hand as she grew a confused look on her face when she saw Chicago and Edris at her doorstep.

"Bitch, don't just stand there like a deer in the head-lights. Let us in," Chicago said quickly as urgency was evident in his voice. Although he was being held at gunpoint, Chicago kept his pimp hand strong.

The girl quickly stepped to the side as requested, and Edris pushed Chicago in. A naked white man came out of the bedroom, and Chicago quickly let him know what time it was.

"Yo, player, you have to bounce. You can come back in an hour and get your rocks off. Sorry about the inconvenience," Chicago said as he looked dead in the man's eyes, letting him know it was time to go. The skinny white man quickly rushed to the room and gathered his clothes. He rushed out in his underwear, obviously scared to death. The sight of two dangerous-looking black men was enough reason for him to get out of Dodge. They watched as he scurried out and then they got straight to business.

"Where the dough at?" Edris asked as he revealed his gun to the whore, making her instantly throw her hands up in fear. She stood there speechless as she tried to understand what was going on.

"Sweetie, go and get the money," Chicago demanded.

"What money?" the girl answered, not wanting to give up the fortune that was hidden in her room's closet.

"Stop playing, bitch. Go and get it and get it quick," Chicago said while raising his voice. He had hidden it there a couple of days back. A true street veteran knew to never put all of his eggs in one basket, so he brought half of the money there.

The girl quickly disappeared into the back room, and Edris pointed the gun at Chicago while frequently peeking at the doorway, waiting on the girl to reenter.

With every passing second, Chicago grew more nervous. He knew how Macy and his crew used to get down before he got into politics, and he didn't want to lose his life for something he wasn't aware of. If he knew that Boomer was the john his bottom whore had robbed, he would have never let it go down. Macy ran the city, and Chicago understood that.

"Listen, I hope we can all look past this once you get the money back," Chicago said, trying to ease the tension. He was unsure of what Edris would do after he retrieved all of the money, which made him very uneasy.

"This is strictly business, Chicago. We don't have a beef with you. We just want the money back, that's all," Edris said as he thought about the task at hand.

Finally the girl came from the back with the book bag where the money was at. She walked over to Chicago and dropped it at his feet. "Here it is, daddy," she said as she looked at him with an intense stare. Chicago didn't pay her any mind, but she was trying to give him a heads-up on what was about to happen.

"It's all here," Chicago said as he looked down at the bag and opened it, so that Edris could see that the bag was full of money. Edris bent down to grab the bag, and Chicago's heart dropped. He saw that his whore was pulling out a small .22-caliber gun from behind her.

"No!" Chicago screamed as he tried to stop her from doing something foolish.

Edris quickly followed Chicago's eyes and looked at the whore, who fumbled with the gun. Out of instinct, Edris swung the gun on the girl and let off a round, catching her square in the chest.

The whore flew back and crashed into the glass coffee table. Her once white robe was slowly becoming maroon red with blood as she lay in the shattered glass with dead eyes. Edris' heart pounded as he looked at the lifeless girl who lay in front of him.

Chicago quickly rushed to her side and grabbed her hand; however, it was too late. She was dead. The bullet went straight to her heart, killing her instantly.

"Damn, man," Chicago said as tears began to well up in his eyes. "She was only seventeen. You killed my baby girl," Chicago said as he quickly wiped the single tear away. Edris didn't know what to say; he just stood there and looked into the girl's face. She looked so much younger to him at that point. It seemed as though her youthfulness shone through even more now that he had killed her.

"Damn," Edris whispered as he closed his eyes and shook his head.

Chicago kissed the girl's forehead and slowly turned and looked up at Edris with hatred in his eyes. Chicago wanted to kill him, and his emotions got the best of him. He reached for the gun that was on the floor a couple of feet away. He was determined to kill Edris for killing his whore, but Edris wasn't letting that happen.

Edris let two rounds off in Chicago's back, causing him to collapse on top of his dead girl. He, too, was dead at the hand of Edris. Edris quickly grabbed the bag full of money and headed out the door, using his shirt to turn the knob.

He hurried down the stairs and into the car. Edris' hands were shaking, and he was frantic as he tried to get off of the scene as quickly as possible. He had murdered before, but that particular one didn't sit right with him. He never murdered a kid, and to know that the girl was only seventeen weighed heavily on his heart.

As he turned off the corner, he noticed something in his rearview mirror. A cop had pulled behind him. He grew nervous as he suddenly remembered that there was a hooker in his trunk. "Fuck!" he said as he hit the steering wheel violently and peeked in his rearview mirror once again.

The cop hit his lights and sounded his siren. At this point, Edris' heart was pounding so hard it seemed as if he had a baboon in his chest trying to get out. Edris slowly pulled over and began to try to regain his composure. He wiped the sweat from his brow and cleared his throat as he waited for the police officer to approach his car.

"Hello, Officer," Edris said as he looked over his left shoulder and directly in the cop's flashlight.

"License and registration, please," the officer said. Edris put on a fake smile and reached into his glove compartment. He handed it to the cop.

"There you go, sir," he said.

"I pulled you over because you have a busted tail-light," the cop stated. "I'll be right back."

Edris couldn't do anything but sit and wait as he hoped like hell that the hooker didn't make any noise to alarm the officer. After a few minutes of waiting, Edris noticed two other police cars pull up. He grew even more nervous as he wondered why the officer called for backup. Edris thought about grabbing his gun and shooting it out with the cops, but he chose to relax, knowing that he was outnumbered.

Without warning, Edris had three cops surrounding his car with their guns drawn. "Put your motherfuck-ing hands up where I can see them!" one of the officers yelled.

Edris' luck had run out. Just so happened that the girl in the trunk had busted out the light and managed to squeeze her hand out of the light's opening. When the officer noticed it, he immediately called for backup. One other thing: The girl in the trunk suffocated be-cause of lack of oxygen.

Edris had a murder weapon on him and a dead girl in the trunk; it wasn't looking good for Edris. It was the end of the line for him—and Macy.

Chapter Twelve

Edris sweated profusely as he sat in the interrogation room. Two male cops stood over him as the light from the ceiling seemed to be straight down on his head. He had no options. He was a black man with a dead white girl in the trunk. Not to mention, he had a bag full of money when he was pulled over. Edris' heart began to beat rapidly in his chest as his harsh reality began to set in. The two male cops were breathing down his neck as Edris thought twice about repeating what he just had said.

"What? Say that again?" one of the detectives asked, not believing what Edris just said.

"I said, I have proof that the mayor killed his son," Edris said with watery eyes. The thought of him going to jail for the rest of his life changed his view on things. He knew that things looked bad for him, but with the information he had on Macy, maybe they would cut him a deal. "And I have a tape to prove it." Edris dropped his head in shame as he couldn't believe what he was about to do. He was breaking the code of the streets, and he would forever regret the decision that he just made.

Edris would eventually lead the police to the surveillance tape that showed Macy and his goons entering the hotel room where the homicide happened. Edris had just broken the first rule of the street, and he would forever be labeled a rat.

After that day, Edris was shipped to an unknown location and never seen again, while under the protection of the government. The media frenzy had now been multiplied by ten as the local news turned into national news concerning the crooked mayor known as Macy Sigel.

Within twenty-four hours, an arrest warrant was issued for the city's mayor, Macy Sigel. The media was already in a frenzy, but now it was complete pandemonium. Macy's checkered past began to be questioned, and the media was having a field day with the missing-in-action mayor, who was accused of murdering his own son.

Macy sat in the chair and it seemed like a thousand ideas ran through his mind as he tried to figure a way out of his current predicament. He stared at Jordan, who sat across the room and stared at the basketball game that was on television. Jordan playfully tossed a balled-up piece of paper in the air as if he were shooting a basketball. Macy watched closely and knew that Case would kill him after he retrieved the money, so Jordan was his only hope.

"You got a little bit of game, huh?" Macy said as he released a small smile and hoped that he could ease his way into an alliance with the young kid.

"Yeah, I used to be nice back in the day," Jordan said without any emotion.

"You played ball?" Macy asked, trying to further the conversation.

"Look, I'm not supposed to be talking to you," Jordan answered back as he stopped tossing the paper and finally looked at Macy.

"What? Is the other guy your boss or something?" Macy said, understanding that Jordan had opened a door of opportunity for him to play mental chess.

Jordan instantly frowned at the comment and stuck his chin in the air as if he were trying to seem tougher than he was.

"I don't have a boss. I'm my own motherfucking boss," Jordan answered with hostility in his voice.

"Don't seem like it," Macy said under his breath just before he let out a small chuckle.

Jordan quickly jumped up and balled up his fist and stared at Macy intensely. "Look, I ain't nobody's fucking worker! I'm a fucking boss fo' real. You must not know 'bout me, fam. I'm Jordan Zamora, one of the realest niggas that ever been 'round these parts," the naïve Jordan said, not knowing that he was only making himself look more foolish than dangerous.

"I don't doubt that, youngblood. My apologies," Macy answered smoothly as he smiled and realized that Jordan had messed up by foolishly saying his own last name. Jordan, now satisfied with Macy's new point of view, sat down and focused back on the television.

Macy's mind began to churn even more as the name Zamora sounded very familiar to him. He once knew a Zamora. His name was Tino Zamora, to be exact. Tino used to run packs for him before he started using his own supply and supposedly overdosed.

"You wouldn't happen to know Tino, would you?" Macy asked. Before Jordan could even answer, Macy smiled and continued. "You don't remember me, do you?" Macy said as he slowly nodded his head up and down while gazing at Jordan.

It was 1991, and Macy had just gotten back in town from copping from his out-of-town coke connect. He had twenty kilos of pure cocaine in the trunk of his money-green Benz, and within hours he would flood the city. Although it was mid-summer, he was about to set the city on fire with the grade-A product he possessed. Whoever said it didn't snow in California was a damn lie, and Macy was living proof.

Macy was about to go to the trap spot, but first he had to make a stop. Word got back to him that Tino, a former worker, had passed a week earlier while he was out of town.

Macy pulled up to the small brick house that was in one of the neighborhoods he supplied. Kids played in the streets, and all eyes were on him as he slowly pulled onto the block. When his car parked on the curb, it seemed as if time stood still. The children admired his car and custom gold rims as they began to ooh and ah over the luxury vehicle.

Macy grabbed the box that sat on his passenger side and stepped out of the car. The thick gold rope around his neck seemed to glisten as the sun hit it just perfectly. Macy made his way to the door of his deceased friend to offer his condolences to his wife.

Macy saw a young kid dribbling a basketball on the sidewalk in front of the house and immediately saw the resemblance. The young boy was the spitting image of his father, Tino. Macy walked up to the young boy and looked down at him. The young boy dribbled the ball while keeping his head down, so he didn't notice the man hovering over him. Macy kneeled down so that he could get eye level with the boy.

"You look just like your daddy," Macy said as he released a small grin. He then handed the box of Air Jordans to the young kid. The young boy's eyes lit up at the sight of the expensive shoes that he had always wanted. Macy smiled as he saw the face of the young kid light up with joy.

Macy felt obligated to come see the family of the fallen soldier who he once called a friend. The young boy watched as Macy stood up and walked to the front porch where his mother was waiting. Macy gave the woman a warm embrace. She fell into his arms and cried as Macy ensured her that everything would be all right. He managed to get a smile out of her as he placed his hand on her shoulder and gave her his perfect smile. He then reached into his pocket and slid a bankroll of ten thousand dollars to her. Macy then whispered something to the woman and gave her a light kiss on the cheek.

He walked past the young boy and rubbed on his head as the boy was already trying on the Air Jordans. Just as quick as Macy arrived, he had left. The young boy stared in admiration and watched as the car left the block.

Jordan looked at Macy closer and remembered that day as vividly as Macy told the story. The little boy was Jordan, and he recollected how that money helped his mother get a car and gave her temporary happiness.

"Yeah, your father was a stand-up guy. That was my nigga," Macy said as he couldn't believe the coincidence. Macy also thought about how he ordered Edris to kill Tino and make it look like a drug overdose. Tino was shaving money off of the top of Macy's packs, and Macy acted accordingly. A hot shot of bad dope was forced into Tino's arm for his disloyalty, and it was a part of the game.

Macy was never a firm believer in karma, but at that point, he began to be certain that it existed. Years before, Macy had killed the father of the person who had Macy's life in his hands. Jordan had no idea that he was in the presence of his father's killer, and Macy had no intentions of letting him know, of course. Macy looked at the coincidence of him knowing Jordan's father as a chess move. The mental manipulation had just begun.

Jordan quickly got up and left the room. He almost began to tear up at the thought of that difficult time in his life. He had to get himself together and not let Macy see that he was getting choked up. Jordan began to question his role in the kidnapping. How could he do this to the man who helped out his father and mother?

Macy sat back and smiled as he noticed the change in Jordan's demeanor. He had just planted a seed that would eventually blossom into his escape.

Aries was upstairs staring out of the window and shook her head from side to side in disbelief. *I can't believe this nigga has me playing a kidnapper,* she thought as her trigger finger began to itch. She wanted so bad to go across town and show Case who was boss.

She quickly dismissed the idea when she thought about her family at home. Aries knew that she had put them in a bad situation, and she couldn't wait until the job was over so that it could finally be done and over with. Aries didn't want to admit it, but the feel of a gun in her palms felt good. She thought that she had left her past life behind, but just like always, karma came back around and pulled her back in. She had committed so many murders, had caused so many tears, and now that the tables were turned, she felt the burden that she had placed on so many different people.

Aries began to think about all her girls. They all had one thing in common: they were all dead. She was the last one standing. She thought about the original Mamas: Anisa, Robyn, and the one and only Miamor. She couldn't help but to think that she would follow the same path as all of her girls and end up in an early grave. Aries quickly dismissed that thought once she thought about her son, who she would leave behind if she died. *I am going to be there for him no matter what,* she thought as she continued to stare out the window.

With the Murder Mamas, she had a lot of bad times, but there were good ones, too. She smiled as she thought about the time they were hired to kill a man and ordered to cut his dick off. Even though they were doing the most horrendous things, good memories came from them.

"Haha!" Aries laughed out loud as she thought back to that crazy night. . . .

Aries and her girls had sat at Applebee's dining and having drinks. They were there to discuss their new hit.

"So how much is this nigga trying to pay?" Robyn asked Miamor as she took a sip of her Long Island iced tea.

"The job pays the usual eighty stacks. That's twenty a p—" Miamor stopped mid-sentence and remembered that the caper wasn't going to be split four ways anymore. All the girls' hearts dropped as they realized that this was their first hit since the death of Anisa. A brief moment of silence arose as the harsh reality of the lost member of the Murder Mamas set in. Miamor wanted to be strong for her crew and continued to explain the job.

"Remember Black from South Beach?" Miamor asked in a low voice as she clasped her hands and leaned into the table to be more discreet.

"Yeah, I remember him. He had us take care of that snitchin'-ass nigga a couple years back, right?" Robyn responded.

"Yeah, that's him. He wants us to take care of a nigga named Fabian. Black has a younger brother doing life in the pen for drug trafficking. From what Black told me, his brother weighs like a buck twenty soaking wet. The story is that Fabian was violating Black's little brother in jail, doing him real dirty. You know, raping him and shit.

"Fabian got released from the joint about six months ago and 'posed to be moving major weight around his area. Black wants us to get at his ass. But there's a catch," Miamor said as she quickly glanced around to make sure no one was in her mouth.

"What's that?" Robyn asked.

"He wants us to cut off the nigga's dick before we kill him," Miamor said before she released a small smirk.

Aries and Robyn burst into laughter simultaneously. They knew Miamor had to be playing. The request was too outlandish to be taken seriously.

"Get da fuck out of here, bitch!" Aries said in between her laughter; but when she saw that Miamor's smirk had faded away, she knew that she was dead serious.

"You have to be fucking kidding me," Robyn added as she began to shake her head, not believing what was being asked of them.

"I know the shit sound crazy, but the nigga we supposed to hit was raping Black's brother in the joint. He wants him to feel violated the same way his brother did. He is offering us an extra twenty stacks if we do it his way."

"Twenty thousand?" Aries and Robyn asked at the same time.

"Twenty thousand dollars," Miamor confirmed and nodded her head.

"Ooh, big daddy. You working with an anaconda," Robyn lied as she stroked Fabian's dick with her hand.

Where the fuck are these bitches at? This dirty-dick nigga gon' want me to put my mouth on him in a minute, Robyn thought as she prolonged her extended hand-job on Fabian. She had been getting in good with him for the past week and finally convinced him to go to a motel room without one of his goons tailing him for security.

"Show me what that head game like, ma," Fabian instructed as he placed his hands behind his head and lay back on the bed. Robyn was enraged on the inside. She was pissed because Miamor had told her that they would enter the room five minutes after she went in. It had been fifteen minutes since they entered the motel room.

Where these bitches at? Fuck, Robyn thought as she tried to figure out a way to buy a couple of minutes. Normally she would do whatever she had to do to get the job done, but in this case she had to reconsider. The thought of putting a homosexual pipe in her mouth made her almost gag. Robyn stood up and improvised to stall time.

"I'ma dance for you, daddy. Just sit back and watch," she said as she began to do the belly roll and move her midsection in circles. She raised her skirt and exposed her neatly trimmed vagina. She put her finger in her mouth and then began to rub her clitoris slow and hard.

Fabian was going crazy thinking about going inside of her pretty pink love box. He smiled while stroking his hard dick. He was so hard; veins were sticking out of his dick as the tip of his joint pulsated.

It wasn't Robyn's intention to get aroused, but the size and width of Fabian's big black rod made her dripping wet. *If the nigga wasn't a homo, I might've gave his fruity ass some. That's what's wrong with these*

*bitch-ass niggas now! All the brothers either down-
low booty chasers or just don't got no act right*, she
thought as she let her finger slide into her vagina. She
was so wet; she felt her juices drip onto her inner thigh.

At that point Fabian couldn't take it any longer. He
jumped up and swiftly grabbed Robyn under her butt
cheeks. He quickly lifted her so that she was face level.

"Oh shit!" Robyn yelled as the element of surprise
caught her. Her legs swung freely as her crotch sat dead
in the middle of Fabian's face.

During his stint in the penitentiary he had worked
out extensively; his bulky, muscular physique confirmed that. It was nothing for him to lift Robyn's entire body with ease. He began to work his tongue like a
tornado on Robyn's clitoris.

She couldn't believe the position that she was in. She
only read about shit like that in books. Fabian knew all
the moves to get Robyn to nut. *This nigga sho' can eat
a pussy*, Robyn thought as she gripped his bald head
in pleasure and grinded her hips against his face. The
top of her head kept hitting the ceiling, but she didn't
mind. It was well worth it.

She kept looking at the door, expecting her girls to
bust in at any moment. She had paid for the hotel suite
earlier that day and gave Miamor the extra room key.
Actually, she was hoping that they didn't come in at
that moment because she didn't want Fabian to drop
her while she was so high.

"Let me down!" Robyn said as she tried to get a couple more face thrusts in before it was over.

Fabian slowly let Robyn down and began to take off
Robyn's clothes. He lay on the bed and sat up on his
elbows as he stared at her drenched pussy.

Robyn knew that she had to think quickly because
she was not about to give him a shot at her goods. *He*

ain't sticking that mu'fucka up in me. That's for damn sure.

"Turn around on your stomach," Robyn instructed as she sucked her own nipples.

"What?" Fabian asked in confusion.

"Turn around, nigga! I want to lick yo' ass," she lied seductively.

"What? Don't nothing go by my ass, ma. Come get on this dick and stop playing."

Robyn knew what the deal was, and she knew that he liked what she was proposing, him being gay and all. She just had to play it right. "It will feel good, I promise," Robyn added.

Fabian lit up inside when she first told him to turn around. He just didn't want Robyn to know his little secret. Her request was music to his ears. He hadn't got a rim job since leaving prison. He was itching to get his fetish quenched. Fabian looked in Robyn's eyes and saw that she was serious and quickly flipped his muscular ass around.

Just then, Robyn saw Miamor and Aries slide through the door quietly, both with pistols in their hands. Fabian was so busy smiling and anticipating getting his back slurped that he didn't even see them coming.

"What took y'all bitches so long!" Robyn shouted as she began to put on her clothes.

"What?" Fabian asked as he turned around. But he didn't see what he was expecting to see. He was staring down the barrel of Miamor's 9 mm. Before Fabian could even act in response, Miamor went across his nose with her gun, causing it to split and swell up instantly.

"Tie this mu'fucka up," Miamor instructed calmly as she reached into her bag to pull out the butcher knife.

Fabian instantly began to plead for his life as Aries tied him up to the bedposts.

"Look, I will give y'all bitches anything you want," he pleaded as Aries finished tying him up.

Aries hit him in the eye with the butt of her pistol. "Watch chu mouth!" she said as she watched him grimace in agony.

"Let's hurry up and get this shit over with," Robyn said as she finished putting her clothes back on.

"Okay, here," Miamor said as she handed Robyn the butcher knife.

"I ain't cutting that nigga dick off!" Robyn said as she shook her head from side to side.

"Oh shit! Oh fuck! Please don't cut my joint off. Please! What the fuck did I do to deserve this foul shit?" Fabian said as tears began to form in his eyes and he bucked against his restraints.

"Stop crying like a little bitch! Put a sock in that nigga's mouth," Miamor instructed.

Aries grabbed one of his socks off the floor and forced it down his throat.

"Aries, you do it," Miamor said as she handed her the knife.

"Chu got Aries fucked up. Me not touching he dick, bitch," Aries said as she stepped back away from her.

"Y'all bitches soft! I got to do everything myself! Real bitches do real shit," Miamor yelled as she grabbed Fabian's dick and gave it one good hack. The knife only went halfway through, so she whacked it again, this time cutting it clean off.

Fabian squirmed in pain. The muffled scream was like a lion's roar as his eyes flew open in excruciating pain, while his body writhed violently. Miamor didn't know if it was more painful for Fabian to feel the knife or to see his soldier lying next to him, totally detached from his body. Blood began to cover the sheets, and Miamor hopped off of him.

"I get the twenty stacks for that. Straight up!" Miamor yelled as she grabbed a towel to clean her hands and the knife.

"Fuck that! We are splitting that shit," Robyn yelled as she turned her head to avoid seeing the bloody scene.

"Yeah. We split that!" Aries added.

"You bitches didn't wanna help, so why should I split it up?" Miamor contested.

"I . . ." Robyn paused, and the smell that was in the air almost made her gag. She pulled Miamor into the bathroom so she could tell her about herself. Aries followed quickly, not wanting to miss anything. The three girls huddled up in the bathroom like sardines in a can.

"Yo, why you bugging, Mia? You know the rules. We always split the take evenly," Robyn said with much attitude.

"Why do I have to do the dirty work and split it? Straight the fuck up! You two were scared to cut, but now you want a cut. Fuck that!" Miamor said while snapping her head to the side.

"Miamor, what's gotten into you? You are tripping. You ain't acting the same lately." Robyn scowled.

"It's de nigga she giving she pussy to. He got she head fucked up," Aries said.

"Look, this ain't the right time to be talking about this, so step the fuck off," Miamor said.

"Yeah, she is right. Let's handle this nigga and we will finish this later," Robyn said as she opened the bathroom door and squeezed out.

"Oh shit!" Robyn yelled as soon as she saw what had happened.

"What's wrong?" Miamor shouted as she hurried out of the bathroom. Miamor looked at the bloody bed and saw that it was empty and the door was wide open.

"The nigga got away! Fuck!"

They all rushed to the door and saw the man running butt naked across the parking lot. Aries lifted her gun to shoot at him, but it was too late. He was already out of range.

"Fuck! Fuck!" Miamor yelled as she put both of her hands on her head. She knew that they had just fucked up big time and now no one was getting paid. They all paused for a minute and then watched as the butt naked man ran for his life. On cue, they all burst into laughter, knowing that they would eventually catch up to him. . . .

Aries snapped back to reality and wiped the tear away that had cascaded down her cheek. She couldn't wait until that whole ordeal was over so she could return to normalcy with her family.

Chapter Thirteen

Fatima rubbed her long legs together as she watched Case's naked behind as he walked into the master bathroom. The sweat-drenched sheets clung to her body as she smiled seductively.

"Are you throwing in the towel? We've got years of lovemaking to catch up on," Fatima whined as her lust-filled eyes enjoyed the view of his body. Case was a real man, a man's man, somebody Fatima could hold on to when it felt as if she were grasping at straws in her own marriage. He provided security for her, because when she looked at him, she saw the man she made her son with. Being with Boomer's father, no matter how temporary the relationship was, made Fatima feel better, as if she had taken less of a loss.

"I can't keep up with you, girl. You going at it like we're still seventeen," Case said bashfully as he disappeared into the bathroom.

Being in Case's presence made her feel alive after the death of Boomer. Fatima was living in a dream world, and sooner or later she would have to wake up.

She couldn't wait until Macy was out of the picture. She had given herself to him fully for so many years, and it wasn't until she learned of his betrayal that she strayed. Macy had put a hurting on Fatima, and only revenge would make her feel better. His death would be his own bad karma coming back at him. Macy had arrogantly thought he would get away with the murder of Boomer, but Fatima was going to make sure that he paid for his wrongdoing.

Fatima flipped over on her stomach and crawled to the edge of the bed. She reached for the remote and turned on the TV.

"You need some company in there?" she called out. She was ready to go for round three.

Case chuckled and shouted, "Come join me."

She flipped the covers off to get out of the bed but stopped as her eyes scanned the television. Macy's face was plastered all over it, and she quickly forgot about her sex session. Fatima turned up the volume as her heart began to speed up as she nervously heard the report.

"Case, get out here!" she yelled.

Case came out of the shower just as she was turning up the volume.

"Mayor Macy Sigel has been implicated in the murder of his son. He is wanted for questioning. The police have tried to locate Mayor Sigel, but his whereabouts are unknown. His wife, Fatima Sigel, is wanted for questioning. . . ."

"How do they know about him killing Boomer? Why am I wanted for questioning?" Fatima repeated in a panicked tone.

Case went to the TV and turned it off. "Don't worry about that. He's the mayor and he's been MIA. This was inevitable. Just be cool," Case stated. "They'll find what they're looking for. He'll be in a landfill somewhere soon enough."

"Then we will be okay. We can be together and the death of our son will be avenged," Fatima stated.

Case gave her a skeptical look because he had no intentions of keeping Fatima around. Being with her was only fun when Macy was alive to disapprove of it. He was sexing the wife of his enemy. That fact alone made his dick hard, but the infatuation would be over as soon as Macy was dead.

"Listen, Tima. . . ."

Fatima noticed the look on his face and recognized the regretful tone of his voice. "Case?" she said with an attitude.

"I don't want us to confuse sex with love," Case stated.

Fatima curled her lip in anger. "Oh really?" she asked as she crossed her arms. "I'm not a child, Case. I'm a grown woman and I realize what we are doing. I don't want to be around when your ship sinks anyway. You never know who might get to talking to the police. Once Macy's dead, I'm cashing in the life insurance policy and getting out of this city."

Knowing that women are emotional creatures, Case stopped himself from going off. Fatima didn't know if she wanted to stay or go. She was obviously speaking out of anger. Case realized that letting Fatima down would not be a smart move for him. She had too much on him to let her go, especially on a bad note. There was no way that Case could leave a bad taste in Fatima's mouth without her telling someone what she knew. Fatima could pin Macy's murder on him, and Case was realizing that he would have to keep her close by in order to keep this secret under wraps.

"I'm not telling you to leave, Tima. I'm just saying let's take it slow. I want you around. Matter of fact, it's better for you if you stay," Case said.

"Better for me," she scoffed.

"Yeah. As long as you're under me, I know you're not talking recklessly to anyone. You're more than welcome to cash in your little chips and leave, but if you go that route, I can't guarantee your safety."

"Are you threatening me?" she asked with wide eyes.

"I'm enlightening you," he shot back as he threw on his clothes. Fatima gave him the evil eye as he finished dressing. "I'm going to be back in a few. Stay put."

Fatima's nostrils flared because she felt like Case was trying to play her. They could have been good together, but Case had mistakenly shown his cards. He didn't care for her; this was a Clash of the Titans between Macy and Case. Fatima was just one of the spoils of war. The only reason he wanted her around was so that he could keep her in fear. Fear would keep her in check, but Fatima refused to be handled that way.

She got up from the bed and peered out of Case's bedroom window just as Case pulled away from the condo. As soon as his car was no longer in sight, Fatima sprang to action. She was showered and dressed in less than twenty minutes, but when she went to grab her keys, she noticed that they were missing.

"Fuck. Where are they?" she whispered in frustration as she retraced her steps. "I know I'm not crazy. That muthafucka has my keys."

Refusing to stay put, Fatima called a cab, hoping that it would arrive to pick her up before Case came back. She wasn't explaining anything to anyone. Case didn't want her; Macy had hurt her. Now she was out for self.

Chapter Fourteen

All I have to do is get the life insurance policy out of our safe deposit box and then I'm out of here, Fatima thought.

The honking of a car's horn snapped her out of her thoughts. She grabbed her handbag and shot out of the door.

"First National Bank," she said as she put her over-sized shades over her face. She could feel the cabbie's eyes peering at her through the rearview mirror, and she grew antsy in her seat as she tried not to stare back. She kept her eyes on the passing scenery out of the window.

"Aren't you that lady that they've been talking about on the news? Mayor Sigel's wife?"

"Listen, I'll pay you extra to keep your eyes off of me and on the road," Fatima replied.

"Not a problem," the cabbie replied as he turned off the meter, subconsciously knowing that this fare was not one who needed to be documented.

Her heart beat intensely as soon as she saw the building come into view. "Wait here," Fatima ordered. "I'll be right back out."

She walked inside, trying to keep her head lowered to avoid being recognized by the other patrons in the bank. She stood in line and fidgeted nervously until a personal banker approached her.

"Mrs. Sigel, please, I can help you. You don't have to stand in line," the white man said.

Fatima looked around and then followed the man. "I just need to get into our safe deposit box," she said.

"Not a problem," he replied as he led the way toward the back room where the safe deposit boxes were held.

Fatima reached inside of her purse and removed her key and then handed it to the banker as he located her box and removed it from the wall slot.

"Do you need a private room?" he asked.

"Yes, please," she answered.

Fatima was escorted to a small room and left to tend to her business. She smiled when she removed the life insurance papers and the knots of money that were hidden inside. She stuffed everything into her purse. She was carrying a five thousand dollar bag, but the contents inside were worth more than gold to her. As soon as Macy's body was found, she could file her insurance claim. She was about to cash in on a million-dollar policy.

Fatima exited the room and handed the box over to the personal banker and headed for the door.

"Um, excuse me, Mrs. Sigel. Can I interest you in a high interest savings account?" the banker asked as he walked alongside her.

"No, no, thank you. I'm fine," Fatima replied.

"Please. It will only take a moment of your time, and I promise it will be worth your while," he stated. She heard a slight quiver in his voice and again turned him down.

"Wait! Um, I just need to get you to sign these papers that your husband forgot to sign last time he was here," the banker stated.

Fatima saw the banker's hand shake and thought, *What is going on? Why is he trying to stall me?*

"I really don't have time. Another time, I promise," she said graciously, still trying to be the diplomatic wife in public.

She hurried out of the doors and turned to step toward the cab. Out of nowhere two police cars pulled up wildly, lights flashing and sirens blaring. Fatima froze and her eyes widened in fear like a deer in headlights as two officers jumped out of the car and approached her.

She prayed that they would bypass her, but when she turned back toward the bank and saw the branch manager peering nosily outside, she knew. They had come for her. The bank had been informed that if Macy or even Fatima stepped foot inside, to notify the police.

"Fatima Sigel?" one of the officers asked.

She was so horrified that she couldn't respond. She simply nodded her head in acknowledgment.

"We need to ask you some questions about your husband. Can we escort you down to the precinct?" he asked.

Fatima saw the cab waiting for her and wanted to sprint toward it, but she knew that with four police officers on the scene, she would never escape them. *Oh my God. They know about the kidnapping,* she assumed.

The officer grabbed her carefully by the elbow and nudged her toward his vehicle. He opened the door and folded her into the backseat. They drove to the police station in silence, and the only sound that could be heard was Fatima's shallow, frantic breathing. It took everything in her not to shed a tear.

They took her to a small interrogation room and sat her down inside. Without saying anything, they left the room, leaving her alone and terrified. Her mind began to play tricks on her as she watched the minutes on the clock change.

They know something. Do they know that I'm in-volved? Oh God. I should've never gotten into this. What was I thinking? Macy is too powerful. He has too many friends for me to get away with something like this, she thought as her foot put on a nervous tap dance show as it bounced on the ground.

An hour and a half passed before the door reopened and a police officer stepped inside. "I'm sorry for your wait, Mrs. Sigel, but we have some very important things to discuss with you," he said.

Fatima nodded her head and avoided eye contact with the officer. He walked behind her and looped the table before sitting down across from her. She felt like prey as he watched her silently, and her guilty con-science began to work overtime.

"We have reason to believe that you know where your husband is and that you are involved with his recent disappearance," the detective said. "Now, if you know something you need to tell me, Mrs. Sigel. . . . You could get into serious trouble for withholding information."

Fatima felt the tears stinging her eyes as they accu-mulated. They were too full to contain and inevitably escaped as they rolled down her cheeks.

The officer pulled a handkerchief out of his inside jacket pocket and handed it to Fatima. She accepted it and dabbed at her face as her bottom lip quivered.

"Just tell me what you know," the detective said.

"I didn't want to be involved in it. Case made me. He kidnapped Macy and has him tied up somewhere for ransom. As soon as the money is delivered, he is going to kill him," Fatima sobbed.

The detective sat back in his chair in shock. He turned toward the double-sided mirror and looked at his comrades, who were undoubtedly watching on the other side.

He had definitely gotten more than he had bargained for. He was just there because he thought that a loyal wife was harboring Macy and could point them in the right direction. He was investigating Boomer's murder, but because of Fatima's statement, now he was aware of Macy's dire predicament. She had just added a kidnapping and completely separate case to his load.

As soon as Fatima spoke Case's name, the detective knew who she was talking about. The LAPD had been trying to hem the known but elusive drug kingpin for years.

"What relationship do you have with Case?" the detective probed.

"He's . . . he was my son's father," she admitted.

"So the two of you conspired together to kidnap and murder your husband? Maybe because you were angry with him over something else?"

The questions just kept coming and coming. Fatima made the mistake of not asking for an attorney and just kept answering and answering.

"I didn't want him dead. I swear! I was confused. My son had just been killed. It was a mistake. Please, you have to believe me," she pleaded.

The detective nodded his head and rose from the table. "I'll be right back," he said.

He left the room as Fatima quivered in fear. The detective was met by his captain and a few of his comrades. "Looks like we have a twisted tale of murder, corruption, adultery, and kidnapping on our hands," the captain said.

The detective shook his head. "Who would have thought? She basically just sealed her fate. I had no reason to suspect her of anything until she just opened her mouth. We need an arrest warrant for Case, and we need to find Macy Sigel. She just helped me collar the two biggest criminals in the city."

The detective peered back into the room and then looked back at his captain. "What do you want me to do with her? Should I have the D.A. cut her a deal for cooperating?"

The captain shook his head. He wasn't going to extend any gratitude to Fatima. This was the type of investigation that careers were catapulted off of. "No. Arrest her for accessory to kidnapping. She's the mayor's wife. The press is going to have a field day with this one, boys. Pull out your best suits and make sure your uniforms are clean! We've got ourselves a case!"

Chapter Fifteen

Aries walked into the trap spot and shook her head when she saw Jordan and Harlo playing video games.

"This is all you niggas do. I thought I told y'all that somebody needs to be watching him at all times," Aries shouted. She was tired of their mediocrity. Working with them was like babysitting. It wasn't what she was accustomed to, and she couldn't wait for the job to be over.

"Has he eaten?" she asked.

"Man, I'm not untying that mu'fucka," Harlo stated. "If you want him to eat, you feed him. And I don't work for you, so watch who the fuck you're talking to."

Aries stopped mid-step and turned on her heels. She walked over to Harlo and stood directly between his legs. She bent over, putting her hands on his hands and getting eye level with him. Jordan sat back and watched, unsure of what was about to pop off. He could see the fiery rage in Aries' eyes.

"Let me make one thing clear. I will body you in this bitch," Aries stated. "You better check my resume. The only reason your amateur ass is even breathing the same air as me is because Case recommended you to me. Don't test me."

Harlo gritted his teeth because he wanted to pop off, but he knew his place and remained silent, despite the fact that his pride was urging him to go toe to toe with Aries.

"Do we understand each other?"

Harlo nodded. "Yeah, we understand each other."

Aries could see the malice in his heart, and she addressed it quickly. "Don't let your ego get you murked. Your eyes are giving away your true intentions." She stood and went into the kitchen, all the while ready to put two in Harlo's head if she even heard his feet shuffle behind her.

She went into the cabinets and pulled out a loaf of bread and some peanut butter before making a quick sandwich. Aries walked down the basement steps and walked over to Macy. He watched her silently as she untied his uninjured hand, leaving the other one tied down.

"It's not a gourmet meal, but it'll keep you from starving down here," she said as she placed the plate on his lap.

She sat down on the bottom step and watched him. Macy made no move to touch the sandwich. Aries inventoried Macy's designer suit and platinum cufflinks. Everything he wore was high end, and his demeanor exemplified dignity, power, and prestige. He was not her usual mark. A man like Macy was usually the one who hired her. She found it odd that he had fallen victim and had been put on the flipside of her murder game.

"It's not personal," she said. "I don't have anything against you. It's just business."

Macy scoffed as he stared Aries directly in her eyes. "If it's business, then you should be willing to consider a better proposition. Whatever Case is paying you, I'll double it."

"Just like that, huh?" she asked.

"Just like that," he answered.

Back in the day, Aries would have jumped at the opportunity. She was loyal to the money, and whoever was paying the most was who retained her services, but this time she had other interests involved—her family. No amount of money was worth risking their wellbeing.

"Tempting, but I have to pass," Aries stated. "You can't double nothing. I'm not being paid for this."

"I've never known a Murder Mama to do anything for free," Macy shot back. His statement caught Aries off guard, and she noticed the smug expression on his face. Even bleeding and strapped to a wooden chair, Macy maintained a certain superior swagger.

"You've known who I am all along?"

Macy shook his head and replied, "No, not at first. It took me a while to put the pieces together. I couldn't believe that someone like you had caught me slipping."

Aries chuckled. "Someone like me, huh?"

"I don't know too many bitches that are capable of this. It only made sense. No regular woman could pull off what you did. Murder Mamas have a reputation for being beautiful. Beautiful but deadly," Macy replied. "I've heard the stories."

"Then you should know exactly how this one will end," she replied.

"I do," Macy answered with a nod. "I know how you get down. I also know that my paper is long enough to buy me out of this situation. I met one of your girls years ago. Miamor. I had a job for her, but the price she was asking was too steep for me at the time. Now, no price is too steep, so what is yours? Money makes the world go 'round."

"Under normal circumstances it does, but this time is different. I'm in for a different reason. I had left this life alone. I had lost too many loved ones to continue living my life in the fast lane. Miamor died a while ago, and before her was my girl Anisa, and before her our friend Beatrice. Then I watched this city, your city, sentence Robyn to death. I sat there helpless as they put the needle in her arm. So, despite what you may think you know about me, this isn't who I am anymore. Killing isn't fun for me anymore. I was done with all of this shit until Case came knocking at my door."

"Seems like murder is an itch that you just can't scratch. If this isn't you no more, why didn't you turn him down?" Macy asked.

"I owe Case. A few years ago we messed up an important job of his. If I finish this thing with you, he's forgiving all debts. If I don't, my family is the cost that I pay," Aries revealed.

It was at that moment that Macy realized just how serious this was for Aries, and despite the fact that she was his adversary, he felt a bit of empathy for her.

"Sound to me like Case forced your hand," Macy stated. "He's selling you a dream, ma. How much did Case pay you for the job you botched?" he asked.

"A million," she answered.

Macy shook his head because he knew Case would never forgive a debt so large, no matter what Aries did. He would use that to keep her in his pocket. "You're being naïve, ma. Case ain't dismissing that debt until it's paid—in cash. No matter what he says or what type of work you put in on his behalf, I know Case, and he's going to hold that shit over your head forever."

Aries didn't show Macy her indecision, but he had planted a seed of truth that made her question her decision.

"Only way you're going to relieve yourself of Case's debt is to relieve yourself of Case. That million that he paid you was street money. It takes years for a man in Case's position to accumulate that much dough. He's not just going to let bygones be bygones. You're eventually going to have to kill him anyway. You may as well take me up on my offer and get paid for it," Macy stated matter-of-factly. "If there's one thing that I know, it's that Case doesn't forget anything. You burned him once, as did I. You see where I'm sitting right now. I wouldn't be surprised if he had your family strung up from a telephone pole by now."

Aries cut her eyes sharply at him as she stood abruptly to her feet. Macy had hit a nerve within her and he knew it. She walked over to him and removed the uneaten sandwich from Macy's lap. She retied his arm, handling it roughly as she snatched the rope and tied a knot around his hand.

"We are more alike than different, ma," Macy stated.

"That we are," Aries replied with a soft smile, giving him a tiny glimpse of the delicate woman behind the vicious murderer-for-hire.

"Just think about what I've said. Let me go and I'll have a million dollars wired into a foreign, untraceable account," Macy stated.

Aries smirked. "Stop trying to work me, Macy Sigel. I'm not easily manipulated. I've seen more money than my two hands could count. I'm not infatuated by it. It doesn't make me cum," she stated.

"Then what does?" Macy asked, unable to help himself as he gave her a crooked, sly, seductive grin.

Aries shook her head and rolled her eyes, knowing that it was that same look that had gotten him in his current predicament.

"See, that's what got you into this, fucking your best friend's girl all those years ago," Aries revealed. "Case is bitter over that."

"Is that right?" Macy asked.

"Come on, Macy. You should know that this was about more than the money," Aries shot back.

Macy raised an eyebrow as he replied, "So should you. Case is going to burn you in the end. You should get him before he gets to you . . . or better yet, your family."

Aries walked back over to the stairs and sat back down. On the outside she appeared unfazed by Macy's rant, but inside she was in turmoil. She hadn't taken the time out to check in with Prince because she wanted to stay focused. Aries couldn't allow her other persona to cause her to go soft, which was why she had made no attempts to contact Prince since touching down in L.A. Now insecurities crept in her mind.

He's right. I'm underestimating Case, she thought. *What if he doesn't hold up his end of the bargain? My family could be in danger right now and I wouldn't even know it. Prince hasn't called me either, and that's not like him.* She played a thousand scenarios out in her head, but Macy had planted the seed of doubt, and now it was starting to grow. Anxiety manifested itself and concern plagued her.

Macy smiled in satisfaction. Although he was the one tied up, he felt as if he were in control. With three people holding him hostage, there was no way that he could get himself out of the situation by force. He would have to get inside of their heads, and although Aries had been the hardest to break, he was now mind-fucking her nice and slow.

He had always been a thinker. The ability to outsmart his enemy had always been one of his greatest assets. Macy had discovered Aries' weakness—her family—and now her concentration had shifted.

As long as she's thinking about them, she won't be thinking about me, and I'll be able to talk one of her li'l workers into setting me free.

Chapter Sixteen

Aries grew antsy as she thought of the danger that her family was in. Prince was in no way capable of handling himself against Case's goons. He was a square—a marvelous and prestigious businessman, but a square nonetheless. He didn't have an ounce of hood in him and was completely different than Aries. He was her opposite. His simplicity was what had attracted her to him. Prince had a gentle soul that made him the perfect man for her, but it also made him the perfect target for men like Case.

She paced back and forth in the basement, her body serving as a pendulum as she tried to call her husband. "Shit," she mumbled when she noticed that her battery was dead. She desperately needed to hear from him. So far things were going as planned, but something felt wrong. Something was telling her that it was going a little too smoothly. She tried to power on the phone, pressing the on button repeatedly to no avail.

"You're going to burn a hole in the floor you keep that up," Macy stated as he leaned his head back to rest against the wooden chair. "Why are you doing this, ma? Whatever he has over you, I can help. You're working for the wrong man."

Aries stopped midstep and turned her attention to Macy. She walked slowly over to him, her sexy strut commanding his eyes. She made him look where she wanted him to look: from her hips to her thighs to her toned stomach, then finally to her eyes. Aries commanded him, and she shook her head as she thought, *all niggas are the same.*

She chuckled as she put her hands on top of his arms that were tied to the armrests. She leaned on them, putting pressure on his injured arm and causing him to wince in pain. Aries lowered her face to Macy's and said, "I work for myself, and no matter how much those eyes wander, you'll never be able to afford me, in any way. So keep your eyes off of me and save the bullshit-ass manipulation, before I make it to where you're not seeing nothing or saying shit ever again."

Aries stormed off. *I have to get out of this house. I have to call Prince. I just need to hear his voice and make sure that they are okay,* she thought. She was quickly growing overwhelmed, and it was at that moment that she realized that she had outgrown this lifestyle. Although Aries was an executioner by nature, she no longer wanted to be.

When she emerged from the basement, Harlo and Jordan stood to their feet, waiting to jump at her command.

"Watch him, but don't touch him. I want him in the same condition when I get back. I need to step out for a minute. I won't be gone long. Do not untie him," she said as she pointed a warning finger at them.

"We got it," Harlo spoke up as he held out his hand to reach for the gun that Aries held tightly in her hand.

She passed it to Harlo, and before she walked out of the house she said, "Don't fuck this up."

A worried Aries rushed to her car and skirted off to find the nearest phone. Something inside of her didn't feel right. She felt as if something was wrong. Her intuition was nagging at her, pulling at her heartstrings, and she desperately needed to hear from her family.

She pulled up recklessly to the first gas station she saw and hurried inside.

"I need to use a phone. Is there a pay phone?" she asked.

The clerk pointed her toward the back of the store, and Aries sighed in relief as she hurried toward it. The closer she got, the more anxiety attacked her, until finally her fingers dialed her home number. The phone seemed to ring forever before Prince finally answered it.

"Hello?"

"Prince, thank God," she whispered.

"Thank God? Rachel, what's wrong? Is everything okay?" Prince asked. She could hear the concern in his voice, and she immediately closed her eyes and sighed. She was alarming him, which was the last thing she needed right now. *Get yourself together, Aries,* she thought as she cleared her throat and gripped the phone with both hands as she looked around cautiously.

"Yeah, baby, everything's just fine. It's just so good to hear your voice. My mother is really fading out lately, and I'm just a little on the emotional side," she lied.

"We can fly there if you need us, Rachel. You don't have to go through this alone," Prince said.

"But I do," she said solemnly. "How's my baby? How are you?"

"We miss you," Prince replied.

Aries was so full of burden that she had to cover the phone to stifle her sob. "I miss you both too. It won't be much longer. I'll be home soon. I just need a little bit more time to settle things. I'll be home in about a week or so."

"We'll be expecting you. We love you, Rachel."

Aries wished that she could hear her husband call her by her real name just once, but she knew that it would never happen. Prince would never love her if he knew what she really was. He had fallen for the fictitious character that Aries had created. He had no clue the type of person he was sleeping next to or the ungodly things that she had done. He was supportive and loving. He was perfect for Rachel; Aries he would hate.

She was living a double life, and her two personalities were both strangers to her. She wasn't the same killer she had once been. Becoming a family woman had made her vulnerable. It made her feel, and there was no room for emotions in her profession. She didn't know where she fit, because as much as she wanted to be Rachel Coleman, that persona didn't feel quite right either. Aries was lost. She had become misplaced in a world of lies, murder, and mayhem. In that world, money was the motivation and deception was the new truth.

She had tried to run from the monster that was chasing her, but she could never shake it. Aries was beginning to realize that she was running from herself. She desperately wanted to change the things that she had done, but she couldn't. Instead, she had to be a new woman and change the things that she had yet to do. However, the forces of nature always pulled her back, and this time she felt as though she may not end up on top.

"I love you too," she replied before hanging up the phone.

Harlo and Jordan had been holed up in the stash spot for so long that they felt as if they were the ones being held hostage. They had played the back to Aries, but now that she had stepped out, Harlo took the lead. He was tired of taking orders from Aries. *Bitch is too fucking bossy for real,* he thought.

"I'm about to go get some food while that bitch is gone, cuz. I'm tired of staring at these four walls, and I'm hungry than a mu'fucka," Harlo stated.

Macy noticed the look of uncertainty that crossed Jordan's face. He was shook by the thought of being alone with Macy. He wasn't trying to have the entire setup on his shoulders. He was an accomplice—nothing more, nothing less. "Just wait until Aries get back," Jordan replied.

"Wait for what? When she gets back she gonna be talking that bullshit about me leaving. I can leave and be back before she even gets here. She'll never know I stepped out," Harlo reasoned.

Macy silently hoped that Harlo did indeed leave. Harlo was the smarter of the two. Macy had pegged his grimey character as soon as he opened his mouth. Macy would never try to run game on Aries, and Harlo was too hardheaded to think of the consequences to his actions. Jordan, on the other hand, was vulnerable. He was scared and unprepared for what was going down. Macy was positive that if he could get Jordan alone, he could get himself free.

"That's not a good idea," Jordan disagreed.

"Man, quit being a bitch! You fucking pussy!" Harlo shouted, demeaning Jordan. "You scared of this nigga. I don't give a damn if he's the mayor. He bleed just like you. All you got to do is hold shit down until I get back. Consider it babysitting."

"I ain't scared of nothing. I just think we should stay put," Jordan defended despite the fact that his voice wavered a bit. He knew exactly who Macy Sigel was and how he got down. Silently, Jordan respected the retired gangster, but things were already out of his control. He was fourth in command behind three heartless killers. There was no way he could speak up on Macy's behalf. Case, Aries, Harlo, Jordan: That was his rank in the grand scheme of things, so he kept his mouth shut and hoped that the situation played itself out peacefully. Sigel had put in work and was respected in Cali, so Jordan was realistic about the repercussions of his actions. He knew that even if Macy did end up dead, his legacy would live on, and if Jordan's name was involved, the Grim Reaper would be knocking on his door in due time.

Harlo passed Jordan the gun and threw on his hoodie. "Well, you stay put, and I'm going to go grab some food. Don't do anything stupid! I might bring your bitch ass back something," he stated with laughter as he walked out.

Jordan pulled the spare chair away from Macy and sat down in it as he tried to avoid eye contact.

"Can I get some food or something?" Macy asked, seeing how difficult it would be to get Jordan to jump at his request. Macy could sense fear. Like a true predator, he sniffed that shit right out of the air whenever Jordan was around.

Jordan pretended as if he didn't hear him. The young hustler wasn't trying to converse with Macy. He was oblivious to the bouncing of his leg, but little did he know he was giving himself away. It was a sure sign of his nervousness. It was obvious that he feared Macy.

Jordan was drowning in the streets. He wanted to be a part of the lifestyle, but when it was time to put in major work, he froze. He didn't look at Macy as the mayor. He had heard the stories of how Macy used to get down, and he was intimidated by the street legend. The way Jordan saw it, he was in a lose-lose situation. If things went badly and they were caught, they would receive football numbers for kidnapping a public official. But if things were kept in the street, then Macy's

goons would undoubtedly get at them for the disrespect. There was no way Jordan would have had any
part in this scheme had he been given the full details.
He had just been trying to make a quick dollar, but not
at the expense of crossing a man like Macy.

"I'm not going to bite you, li'l nigga. I just need some
food. I can't get no money delivered if I'm passed out
from hunger," Macy said, breaking the tension in the
air.

Jordan looked at Macy. He tried to play tough, but
the creases of worry in his forehead betrayed him.
Macy could see the fear in him. "Ain't no food here."

Macy countered, "Can I get some water then?" He
was testing the young kid, trying to see how much he
would budge and measuring his gangster. A true goon
wouldn't give a damn about what Macy needed and
definitely wouldn't bend to Macy's requests.

Macy could see the unsure look in the kid's eyes.
"Yeah. I guess that's cool. I'll be right back." Jordan
disappeared up the stairs and returned a few moments
later with a plastic cup filled with water.

He held the cup to Macy's lips and allowed him to
take a couple sips. Macy accepted the much-needed
fluid and then sat back in the chair as Jordan went back
to his own.

"What's your name?" Macy asked.

"Look, man, I'm not for the talking. I'm just sitting
here until Harlo get back," Jordan stated.

Harlo, huh? Macy thought as he made a mental note
of the other kid's name. Jordan didn't even realize that
he had dropped a valuable jewel in Macy's lap, one that
Macy would surely cash in later. Macy was taking that
chip straight to the bank as soon as an opportunity
presented itself. Harlo's mother would be planning his
funeral. Macy knew that the more he kept Jordan talking the easier it would be to get inside of his head.

"Fair enough," Macy stated. "I've just been sitting back watching the entire situation. You've gotten yourself in quite the predicament. The bitch and your homeboy seem like they're running the show. Seems like you want out. This isn't what you bargained for, eh?"

Jordan shook his head but didn't respond. He was edgy and nervous. "When they were talking about a kidnapping, all I thought about was the paper. I had no idea it was going to be you," he stammered.

"I can't fault you for what you didn't know . . . but now you know. It's what you do from this point that determines how things end for you. You and your peoples don't know who you're fucking with," Macy said. The statement was arrogant but true. Harlo and Jordan were clearly out of their league.

"Man, I just want out of this shit," Jordan stated, overwhelmed, as he rubbed his head and stood to his feet.

"Just let me go. Untie these ropes and my beef with you goes no further. You think my people not gonna know who did this? It's only gonna be a matter of time before my shooters come running through that door. Why you think I haven't come off of that cash yet? If I really thought my life was in danger, don't you think I would have paid up by now?" Macy asked. "I'm the only mu'fucka in this house with nothing to worry about."

Jordan's anxiety turned to panic as he kicked his chair over in frustration. "Fuck, man! Fuck! This nigga always dragging me into some bullshit," he uttered.

"He dragged you into it; now I'm offering you an out. Let me go and walk away," Macy stated.

"I can't just walk away. If Case or Harlo find out I just let you go, I'm dead anyway," Jordan said. "Ain't no running from a nigga like Case. If I just disappear,

I'm gonna look hot and he's gonna come after me. If I cross you or I cross Case . . . either way I'm still fucked. I need your help, man. I want to let you go, but I can't make it look like I went against the grain."

"The game is called self-preservation. Your homeboy and homegirl . . . they're dead. These ropes can only hold one man. I've got goons for days," Macy stated. "Look, you make it look however you need to, as long as I'm walking out of here," Macy replied.

"Nobody's gonna blame you for playing it smart and saving yourself. You don't have much time to decide. When my shooters come through, they're not gonna be asking questions, and my offer for your safety will expire."

Jordan went to the stairs and looked up to make sure that no one had come back into the house. "Look, I'm going to let you go, but I need your word that you won't send nobody after me. I didn't want shit to do with this."

Macy nodded his head. "You have my word. As a matter of fact, you need to be working for me anyway. With Case you'll get nowhere fast. Untying these ropes and coming to play on my team will be the smartest decision you ever make."

"Okay, okay," Jordan mumbled as he thought of a plan that would make him look innocent on both sides. "Look, I'm going to untie you, but I need you to help me make it look like you got loose on your own." Jordan took the clip out of the 9 mm gun he held. "I want you to hit me with the gun and rough me up a little bit so that they will think you overpowered me," he explained.

Macy nodded and said, "I got it. Just hurry up and untie me before they get back. I'm gonna remember this, fam."

Jordan hurried and bent down to free Macy. He placed the empty pistol in Macy's lap as he feverishly freed Macy's injured hand from the tight binds. "You're losing a lot of blood. You're going to need to go to the hospital," Jordan observed as he worked as quickly as possible. He continued to check over his shoulder to make sure that Aries and Harlo had not returned.

As soon as Jordan released his good hand, Macy grabbed the gun off of his lap and smashed it into Jordan's head. Stunned, Jordan fell backward to the ground. Macy pulled the other ropes from his hand and attacked Jordan mercilessly, breaking his face with the steel of the pistol. He hit him repeatedly, until he was defenseless, and then reached into Jordan's pocket for the clip. He popped it into the gun, cocked it back and . . .

BOOM!

Without hesitation, he blew a hole in Jordan's head.

BOOM! BOOM!

And he put two in his chest just because.

Macy never had any intentions of putting Jordan down with him. He was willing to say anything to get himself out of the predicament. Not only did Jordan disgust him for participating in his kidnapping, but the young thug was weak-minded and didn't stand behind his own decisions. Jordan was disloyal and was willing to jump ship as soon as trouble presented itself. He was the worst kind of street nigga there was—indecisive, incompetent, and easily shaken. Macy could never invite someone like him on his team. He only surrounded himself with thorough individuals, and Jordan was weak.

Macy felt no guilt about ending the young boy's life. *I did him a favor by killing him quick. Once Case found out I was free, he would have done much worse,* Macy thought, knowing exactly how his old comrade got down. He dug into Jordan's pockets and removed a set of keys and a cell phone before creeping up the stairs. He let the gun lead the way as he made his way out of the house.

Chapter Seventeen

Case looked down at his watch and then he picked up his cell phone to double check. Edris still had not called him so that he could drop off Macy's ransom. Case knew that he was playing with fire by kidnapping a mayor, let alone a former drug boss. Case didn't want to admit it, but he needed the ransom money. His drug business was going under and his coke connect's prices kept getting higher, but the city's demand was getting lower. Not a good combination.

Case grew more anxious as the ticking minutes went by. He couldn't wait to put the order in to kill Macy, but he needed that money before he could make it final.

Case needed to calm his nerves, so he went over to what he called his candy jar and emptied its contents on the table. A big white pile formed, and he dipped his nose in it and sniffed. He quickly jerked his head back and closed his eyes, trying to prevent his nose from running.

Case began to pace his floor back and forth as the potent coke began to work its magic. Paranoia began to sink in, and Casey grabbed his assault rifle from the closet and peeked out of the window every couple of seconds, anticipating some of Macy's goons.

"Mu'fuckas ain't gon' catch me slipping," he said loudly as he dipped and snorted another small pile. His phone rang, which startled him as he snapped his head in the direction of the counter where his phone vibrated and danced around. He rushed over to the phone and picked it up.

"Hello!" Case yelled into the phone as sweat beads began to form on his forehead.

"We here. We got him," the other voice said on the phone. Case smiled and then closed down the phone. He had just gotten confirmation that his henchmen had Aries' unsuspecting husband in their presence.

He'd sent a couple of his most ruthless goons for Aries' family, and he knew that they wouldn't hesitate to pull the trigger if needed. Case's thoughts began to race and the thought of Macy being a mayor and being successful burned him up on the inside. He then began to think about how Macy had taken Fatima away from him.

This all added fuel to the fire as his trigger finger began to itch. He wanted Macy dead. Fuck the ransom money and fuck waiting; Case was ready for blood. Case's once slow pace back and forth across the floor now became a rapid stride. Case took off his shirt because of his rising temperature.

"He gon' take my bitch?" Case asked himself, talking out loud. "Do he know who the fuck he's fucking with?" The more time that passed, the more the coke kicked in and the more Case's blind rage grew.

Case, out of pure adrenaline, raced out of the door with his assault rifle in hand. He headed over to the trap house so that he could put a bullet in Macy's skull personally. He was at a point of no return. He got into his big, tinted Hummer with the rifle in his lap. He cranked up the music and headed to the hood. He was about to end it once and for all.

***

Fatima sat in the holding cell and buried her face in her hands. Camera flashes were nonstop, and the chatter in the room was gradually rising. A cop had tipped the press about the mayor's wife being held in custody, and within minutes, the precinct was crawling with news reporters and journalists trying to get a jump on the story.

Fatima cried her eyes out as she sat on the cold, hard bench, regretting everything that she had done. She had put herself in a losing position and knew that her life would never be the same. The police promised her that by helping them it would "look good" for her when she went to trial for conspiracy to kidnap.

The reporters called for her, but Fatima didn't budge. She was too ashamed to show her face. She had shamed her family name, and she would go down in the record book as a traitor.

"Mrs. Sigel! Mrs. Sigel! Did you set up the mayor to get kidnapped?" one reporter asked as he held his recorder through the cell's bars.

"Are you connected to known thug Casey 'Case' Rogers?" another reporter asked.

Fatima's tears flowed nonstop, and the reporters' questions drove her overboard. She revealed her face, which had mascara-filled tears falling.

"Get the fuck out of my face. Fuck all of you! You have no idea what the fuck I have been through!" she yelled as she walked to the bars and went on a vicious rant. Spit flew out of her mouth as she gave them a venomous tongue-lashing.

The sergeant on duty felt that it was enough and ordered everyone out of the holding cell area. As the reporters filed out of the area, they all snapped photos, trying to get the mayor's wife in a crazed state.

"No, don't leave! Y'all want a show. I'ma give y'all ass a fuckin' show," she said while spitting on them as they left. Her usual sophisticated and uppity demeanor had totally vanished, and she acted more like a hoodlum than a lady.

Fatima plopped down on the hard bunk bed and breathed heavily as she shook her head from side to side. She had sold her soul to the devil—and the price was cheap.

Case finally reached the trap spot, and he had sniffed at least another gram of coke on his way there. Another car was pulling up just as his was. Case hopped out of the truck with a handgun and saw Harlo getting out of the car with a bag of fast food and drinks.

"What the hell are you doing? You are supposed to be inside!" Case screamed as anger entered his body.

Harlo saw the look in Case's eyes and froze in his tracks, not knowing what to say or do. "I . . . I was just . . ." Harlo stuttered as he couldn't find the words to explain.

Before he could get a clear word out of his mouth, Case aggressively slapped the food out of his hands.

"You just what? Nigga, get in the house and do what I pay you to do, li'l nigga! Can't believe this bullshit!" Case spat as his bloodshot red eyes put fear in Harlo's heart.

Harlo nodded his head and entered the house through the back door. Case followed close behind.

"Yo, where is Aries?" Case asked as he scoped the house.

"Don't know. She was here when I left," Harlo said as he too looked around the house.

"Where's Macy?" Case asked as he frowned and gripped his gun tightly.

"He downstairs with Jordan," Harlo said as he stood at the basement's door and looked down. A bad smell like feces reeked from the basement, and Case immediately frowned.

"Yo, Jordan!" Harlo called down the stairs, but got no response. "Yo, Jordan!'" he yelled this time, but even louder. He again got no response. and his antennas immediately went up, sensing that something was wrong.

Case also grew suspicious and headed down the stairs where Macy was supposed to be held captive. They both rushed down the stairs, and the body that was sprawled on the floor startled them. Harlo's eyes immediately shot to the area where Macy was supposed to be and dropped his head when he saw no one there. He knew that he had fucked up big time.

"Where the fuck is he?" Case asked as he stormed through the basement and did a full circle. Macy was long gone.

"Damn, Jordan," Harlo whispered as he kneeled down and closed the dead eyes of his childhood friend.

"Fuck that li'l nigga! Where is Macy? That's what you need to be worried about," Case said as he flipped open his cell phone to call Aries. Case put the phone to his ear while he paced back and forth. Finally Aries picked up.

"Hello," Aries answered.

"Please tell me that Macy is with you," Case said in between clenched teeth.

"What the fuck are you talking about?" Aries asked as she was pulling into the driveway of the trap house.

"Fuck!" Case yelled as rage overcame him. "Where the fuck are you?" he asked as he gripped his phone so tightly that it was on the verge of breaking.

"I'm walking in," Aries said as she began to panic. She wasn't afraid of Case personally, but the thought of her family being hurt by him petrified her. Aries hurried in and jumped at the sound of a gun blast.

Case stood over the two dead bodies with a smoking gun. He was so mad at the incompetence of his goons that he decided to lay down Harlo as well. Case stared down at the bloody hole that rested square in the middle of Harlo's skull. A small red puddle began to form underneath Harlo's head, and Case was at a point of no return. The mixture of the cocaine and blind rage had turned him into a madman, and he was out for blood. His deep hatred for Macy only made his blood boil more at the thought of him escaping from his clutches and subsequently winning—again.

Fatima breathed heavily, and everything seemed to be going in slow motion to her. Dried-up tear stains were on her face as her hands shook nervously and uncontrollably. She thought about her only child, Boomer, and smiled briefly as she thought about how innocent he was as a child. He was her baby, and somehow she had failed him. She let him transform to the weak-minded young man he had become.

"I'm so sorry, baby. Momma is so sorry," she whispered as she closed her eyes, only imagining his smile. Fatima's mind then drifted to her husband and how she had intimately betrayed him. She couldn't accept or forgive him for killing her son, but she understood why he did it. Boomer was already on a destructive path, and she knew that eventually Boomer would have killed Macy because of his deep-embedded animosity toward him.

Fatima thought back to the day that they got married and once again smiled. It was such a beautiful day. It was the most memorable day of her life, and if she could, without a doubt, she would go back to that happy time. "I love you, Macy," she whispered as she held her head in shame for crossing him. She let her emotions get the best of her and didn't think logically. She had seen the murderous look in Case's eyes when they discussed Macy, so she had a good hunch that her husband was a dead man.

Fatima tightened the belt that hung from the water pipe above her cell. She wobbled as she tried to balance herself while standing on the bunk bed. She then tied the other end of the belt around her neck tightly. She didn't have a lot of slack in the belt, but it was enough to do what she planned to do.

"Boomer . . . Macy . . . here I come," she said, assuming that Macy was already dead. Fatima took a deep breath and said a quick prayer before stepping off of the edge of the bed. Her legs kicked violently and she involuntarily reached for the belt around her neck, trying to release herself. Her eyes began to roll to the back of her head while her face turned blue. It seemed as if her whole life flashed before her eyes as she choked to death.

After a minute of struggling, her body finally stopped moving and she swung lifelessly back and forth in the middle of the jail cell. She would join her son in the afterlife, not in heaven, but most likely hell.

Chapter Eighteen

Macy dragged his injured arm, grimacing in pain as he rushed out of the house. He saw the Acura TL sitting in the driveway and quickly got inside. He ensured that the safety was off of the gun and placed it in the passenger seat before pulling away. The tires squealed as he pulled off recklessly, trying to get as far away from the trap house as possible. He picked up his phone and dialed Big E.

"Hello?"

Macy frowned when he didn't recognize the voice that picked up.

"Yeah, put E on the phone," Macy stated abruptly.

Big E sat behind the interrogation table sweating bullets. He was now working hand in hand around the clock with the authorities trying to capture Macy. He had hoped that Macy wouldn't call again, but as soon as the phone rang, he knew that the time for the ultimate betrayal had come. Big E's guilt ate away at him, but his back was against the wall. He had started the process of double-crossing his close friend, and there was no turning back now. He was loyal to Macy and loved him like a brother, but he had been caught red-handed with a dead white woman in the trunk of his car. The City of Angels was going to turn devilish on him and fry him if he didn't talk his way out of the situation.

"It's show time. You need to find out Macy's exact location so that we can pick him up," the detective whispered as he muted the line and held out the cell phone
for Edris. "I know this is stressful, but you need to
sound as normal as possible. Your life depends on it."

Edris wanted to tell the police to go to hell, but he
was no longer in a position to be cocky. He took the
phone, all the while shaking his head in disgrace.

*If the shoe was on the other foot, Macy would do the
same,* he thought. Even his mind was playing tricks on
him. The police had drilled that same phrase into his
head for so many hours that Big E had started to repeat
it. He was using anything he could to justify his actions.

Macy had never treated Edris negatively, and embraced him as family. There was no excuse for the
snake move that Big E was pulling, and deep down
he knew it, but he was a desperate man and he was
trapped. He had his own family to think of, and as the
face of his wife flashed through his mind, he felt bur-
dened by his position in the streets. It was true that he
had a responsibility to Macy and that he had stepped
into the game willingly, but it was also true that he had
a responsibility to his wife at home. His family had to
come first, but it didn't make what he was about to do
any easier. He wished that things could have played out
differently, but this was the hand that Edris had been
dealt. He was just playing it the best way he knew how.

A long silence filled the line as Macy waited impatiently for Edris to come to the phone. He found it
extremely odd that someone else had answered in the
first place. In all the years that Macy had known Edris,
he had never allowed anyone to answer on his behalf.
That line was secure and untraceable. Macy had en-

sured that what was spoken between him and Big E remained confidential. He made a mental note to get on Big E for allowing anyone else access to the phone.

Finally Big E came to the phone. "Macy, where are you? I've got that drug money for you," Big E stated.

Macy frowned at his tone, noticing a slight nervousness in his friend's voice. "What?" he stated, disapproving of how recklessly Big E was talking.

"Where are you? I can come to you right now. I killed the bitch that robbed Boomer before you could do it," Big E stated. Macy didn't like how anxious Edris sounded, and a hollow pit filled his stomach. He hoped that the gut feeling of betrayal that he had gotten was wrong, but deep down he knew what was up.

"I don't know what you're talking about, E, but I'll see you around," Macy stated. He couldn't hide the hurt in his voice. Big E had been his man a hundred grand, and now he was state's evidence. Without saying another word he hung up the cell.

Fuck! Everything is out of control. I know Edris is caught up with the police. Stand tall, my nigga. Don't shut me down because of your fuck-up! Shit is probably all in the media, Macy thought, knowing that once reporters got word of what was going on, things would become hectic for him.

Macy quickly flicked on the radio, turning to the local station that reported the news.

"Mayor Macy Sigel is wanted for the murder of his son. The mayor disappeared days ago, just before the police received a tip from an informant that Mayor Sigel was responsible for the shooting of his eighteen-year-old son. Citizens are asked to be on the lookout for the mayor, and if he is spotted, the police ask that you call 911 immediately with his whereabouts. . . ."

Macy turned off the radio knowing that the only person who could have given the police that information was Big E. He had turned snitch and had given the police the smoking gun that they needed to prosecute Macy. *I've got to get to my paper and get the fuck out of here,* he thought as he headed toward his house.

Macy rushed to his side of town, being careful not to draw any attention to himself. His arm felt like a dead limb as the blood crusted around the bullet wound, but he ignored the pain. The first thing on his agenda was to get to his safe.

There was no way Macy could beat a case when the entire city was behind him. He was lucky to even be elected. The city of L.A. had built him up, and now it was time to tear him down. It was the way of the land. No one in La-La land got to live in a dream world forever. Macy was in a nightmare that he couldn't wake up from.

He pulled onto his block and immediately hunched down in his seat when he noticed the unmarked police cars parked on his street. They would have been barely noticeable to the other residents, but to someone like Macy they stuck out like a sore thumb. He was too seasoned not to pick up on the presence of the LAPD.

"Fuck!" he whispered as he pulled into one his neighbor's driveways and turned around. He checked the rearview mirror religiously as he pulled off, hoping that he hadn't been spotted. Macy was at a dead end, and without any funds he was helpless. He was in pain, and for the first time since he was a young kid hustling ounces, he didn't know what to do. His back was against the wall, and the fact that he was injured badly only complicated things further.

I've got to stop this bleeding, he thought. This was the first time since becoming a public figure that Macy hated the attention. Everyone in the city knew who he was. It was going to be hard for him to go anywhere unnoticed.

I need help. I can't get out of this on my own, he admitted to himself. He grabbed the cell phone that he had stolen from Jordan and dialed an old friend, Matthew Hayes, one of California's state senators.

"Senator Hayes' office," the receptionist answered.

"Yes, this is Hank Dillard out of Washington. I need to speak with Senator Hayes immediately," Macy stated, pretending to be one of Matthew's golfing partners who he had become acquainted with over the years. Macy knew that Matthew would never refuse a call from his dear old friend.

"Hank, what can I do for you?" Matthew stated jovially.

"Matthew, listen to me closely, because my entire life is depending on you right now," Macy stated.

He heard the unsure pause from Matthew. Silence sometimes could speak volumes, and before the senator could hang up, Macy added, "Please. Hear me out."

"Macy, where are you? You're wanted by the entire fucking city," Matthew said. "How the hell did you get yourself into this mess?"

Macy shook his head knowing that he was in dire straits. "I need help, Matthew. I need some money. Enough to get me out of town," Macy stated.

"I can't, Macy," the senator replied in a low whisper.

"Why can't you, Matt? Huh? You owe me. I've kept a lot of secrets for you over the years; a lot of secrets that could have ruined you. Remember that hooker down on Sunset? I remember her, so I know you do. It was your dick she was sucking on, right?" Macy asked harshly, pulling cards that he knew were wrong and crossing his boundaries.

He was playing dirty, bringing up things that he had promised to never speak of again. Macy felt like he was going down, and he needed help from those who he had helped over the years. Nothing was off-limits at this point.

"Yeah, I remember, Macy," the senator replied with an exasperated sigh. "But you are hot right now. This thing with you and your son is all over the national news. I can't be seen with you and you know it. It's not personal, kid. I've embraced you since you were first elected. Hell, I endorsed you when you were running, but this thing that you've gotten mixed up in crosses the line. I'm just protecting my career."

Macy sympathized with Matthew. The aging senator was a legend in California. He had been in politics for thirty years and had welcomed Macy, showing him the ropes. Macy had learned a lot from his old friend and had garnered many valuable connections because of him, but the one lesson that he remembered most was self-preservation.

"You owe me, Matthew, and now it's time to pay up. I'm not trying to force your hand, but if I have to I will," Macy said, sending a blatant threat.

The senator sighed deeply because he realized that he was in bed with the devil. "You can't come here, but I'll send someone to you. Locker 287 at the train station. Find it and there will be seventy-five thousand dollars inside. That should be enough to help you get out of town. I can't risk hand delivering it to you," Matthew stated.

"I understand," Macy replied.

"Macy, this will be the one and only time I extend this type of favor to you. I refuse to let a punk like you hold anything over my head. Consider this the price I pay for your silence. I wish you luck, but do not call this office again," he said.

"How quickly can you get the money delivered?" Macy asked, disregarding the senator's statement.

"Give me two hours," he replied.

Macy hung up the phone feeling slightly more confident. Seventy-five thousand wasn't much, but it was enough to help him get by temporarily. Once he was out of California he could come up with more cash, but first he had to ensure his freedom and get as far away from L.A. as possible.

Chapter Nineteen

Aries felt extreme relief after hearing her husband's voice. Knowing that her family was waiting for her to come home gave her motivation to finish the job at hand quickly and efficiently. She was tired of the debt that Case was holding over her. After this they would be done and he would have no business with her.

I'm going to walk away from this life once and for all. I'm tired of living this way, she thought as she pulled back up to the trap house. Aries used to enjoy killing, but her heart wasn't in it anymore. Aries had grown roots back in Barbados, and she realized that living life in the fast lane wasn't worth the risk. She would much rather be living her boring, average, normal life with her family.

She frowned when she noticed that there were no vehicles in the driveway. "I told these stupid-ass niggas not to go anywhere," she mumbled as she parked curbside and turned off her engine.

She hurried into the house. "Yo, I'm back!" she shouted as she looked around, trying to find anything peculiar. There were always supposed to be two people present in the trap house: one to stay on the main level of the house to be the lookout, and one in the basement watching Macy.

When Aries went from room to room and noticed that there was no one standing watch, she rushed down the basement steps.

"Fuck!" she shouted when she saw Jordan's body sprawled across the floor. She kicked the boy's dead body in utter frustration. She wanted to call Case to tell him what had gone down, but feared the wrath that he would dispense on her family.

I have to find him and finish this job before Case finds out Macy's missing. Aries rushed out of the house to scour the streets for Macy. Her wellbeing depended on his demise, so she couldn't stop searching until he was no longer in existence.

Macy pulled up to the large grocery store and parked the car as he eyed the entrance. He still had an hour to wait before he could pick up the money, but it felt as if he would pass out at any moment from the pain of his gunshot wound. Macy was desperate for some aid. His inured arm was becoming unbearable, and he was well aware that he wouldn't get far in his current state. Macy knew that he was taking a risk by going into the mega chain shopping center, but he had to nurse his arm.

He noticed a bum pushing a cart outside of the building. It was filled with empty pop cans as the raggedy man went from trash bin to trash bin searching for anything that he could find valuable. Macy pulled up to him and hit his horn lightly.

BEEP! BEEP!

The bum was so used to being invisible to the general public that he didn't even look up and kept on strolling while singing a tune to himself.

"Hey, my man," Macy called out in a hushed tone as he lowered his head so that he could see out of the passenger window.

The bum stopped walking and stuck a finger in his own chest. "Who, me?" He looked around to see if there was someone standing behind him.

"Yeah, you. You look like you could use a little bit of help," Macy said.

The bum walked up to the car and bent his head inside. "Hey, you that . . . that mayor! Aye! You the mayor! Look at this! The mayor! Stopping to talk to li'l ol' me!"

"Shh!" Macy whispered as he motioned his hands for the bum to keep it down as he looked in his rearview to see if the bum had garnered any unwanted attention. "Shh! Keep it down! Calm down!"

"Oh, my bad. My bad. Ol' Rosco get crazy sometimes. Ain't this some shit! The mayor talking to me. What a day, what a day!"

"Look, man, quiet down," Macy stated. "Get in the car. I've got a proposition for you."

Rosco the bum entered Macy's vehicle, and Macy pulled to the back of the parking lot. Rosco noticed that Macy was injured. "Aww, shit. Who shot ya?" he asked.

"You asking a lot of questions, fam. Listen, I have a proposition for you. As you can see, I'm hurt real bad. Now, I can't walk up in this store looking like this, so I need someone like you who can go in there for me," Macy explained.

"No problem. Buy me a beer and I'll go in there and buy the whole sto' for ya," Rosco stated.

The man's over-the-top personality would have been hilarious if Macy weren't in such dire straits.

"Nah, I don't want you to buy it. I need you to steal me a few things," Macy said.

"Steal! What the mayor got to steal fo'?"

"Look, Rosco? That's what you said your name was?" Macy asked. Rosco nodded and Macy continued. "If you go in the store, grab a few items for me and then ride with me across town, I'll give you this watch. It's worth about five thousand dollars. That'll buy you more than a bottle of beer."

"Five thousand dollars?" Rosco asked incredulously.

"Five thousand dollars," Macy confirmed.

"Aww shit! Rosco working for the mayor. I tried to tell these niggas I'm on the come-up! Look, though, I think I can help you out on a few things! Gotta clean up these streets, Mayor Sigel. These bitches funky than a mu'fucka. Stanking just like piss. Put your face on the ground to take a quick nap and you wake up smelling like straight toilet bowl."

Macy couldn't help but chuckle as he pointed at the entrance of the store. "Let's work on this first. We'll worry about the rest later. I need some peroxide, gauze, antibiotic ointment, Tylenol, a new shirt, a baseball cap, and tape. Get me enough to last a few days."

Rosco nodded. Macy pulled up to the door and Rosco hopped out and entered the store.

Macy waited impatiently in the car until Rosco finally emerged from the store. Macy pulled off as soon as Rosco was inside. He drove a good five miles before he pulled over at a small gas station.

"You get everything?" Macy asked.

"Yeah, everything is everything," Rosco replied. "Can I get my watch? I got to get going. I've got places to be."

Macy looked at Rosco sternly, silencing him instantly. He slid the watch from his wrist and handed it over to Rosco, standing true to his word. It was a gift from Fatima anyway, and Macy wanted nothing that would remind him of her or the fact that she was sleeping with Case.

"Nice doing business with ya," Rosco stated as he exited the car.

Macy went into the gas station, keeping his head down, and headed directly for the bathroom. Once he was safely inside, he locked the door and removed his bloodied shirt. He winced in pain as he flexed his hand and put it under the running faucet. Pink swirled in the bottom of the sink as Macy cleaned his wound. He gritted his teeth to keep from yelling out in pain. The bullet was still lodged in his hand, but he just had to bear with it until he could get real medical help.

The peroxide bubbled like lava as he poured it over the gaping hole in his hand. He then wrapped it in gauze and put on the clean button-up shirt before going back to his car. He looked at the clock, noticing that he only had an hour to blow before it was time to go to the locker.

He headed for the train station, and when he arrived, he smirked knowing that he would be lost in the hustle and bustle of the crowd. He pulled the baseball cap down over his eyes and then walked into the train station, discreetly watching his back as he cautiously made his way to the locker. He located it and noticed that the key was still in the keyhole. He looked around before reaching inside and removing the briefcase that lay inside. He rushed outside, threw the money in the trunk, and then pulled smoothly away. Macy didn't know where he was going, but he knew that his future was not in L.A.

"How could you have been so stupid?" Aries fussed at herself. "Stupid! Stupid!" She hit the steering wheel for emphasis each time that she spoke. Aries felt panicked because she knew that actually finding Macy was an impossible feat. L.A. was a big city, and Macy Sigel was a man on the run. There were a million and one hideout spots that Macy could find to stay off of her radar.

Aries had never had a job go so terribly wrong, and the chaos was slowly driving her mad. There was no way that she could go back to Case empty-handed. As soon as he realized that Macy had escaped, there would be hell to pay.

She had checked everywhere and was slowly but surely running out of options. Things were looking dismal, and her heart sank when she finally realized that she must give up. She had fucked up. Her skills and thirst for blood weren't what they used to be. Aries was in over her head, and without the other Murder Mamas around to keep her together, she was slowly going crazy.

Murder was a heavy burden to carry alone. Before, she had relied on a sisterhood to shoulder the pain. They distributed it evenly amongst themselves, convincing each other that it was completely justified, that their victims deserved whatever death sentence they received, but Aries had worked this job alone, and it was starting to get to her.

"This isn't for me anymore," she whispered.

Just as she said the words, Case's number popped up on her phone. She knew that she should answer it, but instead she allowed the call to be forwarded to voice mail.

I'm out, she thought. Instead of carrying on her search for Macy, she busted a U-turn and headed for the airport. Macy was not a dumb individual, and Aries knew that with his connections and resources, finding him would be like searching for a needle in a haystack. So instead, she decided to flee. It was the only option that she had.

She was going home to her family and relocating them. Aries didn't care how far she had to go to ensure that her husband and son remained untouched. Some may feel as though she punked out, but Aries was just empty. She had done too much and seen too much over the years to even continue.

She understood that Case would seek her, but she hoped to get a head start on him. By the time he realized what had occurred, she would be halfway across the world, and her family would be moved to a completely new place. This time she would make sure that Case or no one else would be able to find her, and that meant staying out of L.A. for good. If the day ever did come when he darkened her doorstep, she would greet him with lead this time around.

It was time for her to tell the truth to her husband about who she really was. She would not be able to convince him to relocate without telling him the reason why. Aries could no longer lead the double life. It was too time consuming, and she had to remember so many lies that it was driving her crazy. If Prince knew it all, he would either judge her for her sins or help her through them. She hoped he loved her enough to help her cleanse her soul.

Aries picked up her phone and dialed her husband's number. She was so nervous that she called the wrong number before finally getting it right.

"Hello?" Prince answered.

"Prince . . . I need to talk to you," Aries said as she sniffed as tears began to fall. She was overwhelmed and her back was pressed against a wall. Silently she knew that getting married and having a child was a huge mistake. She loved them too much, and that made her weak. She constantly feared for their safety, and when dealing with a man like Case, it became an unbearable load to carry.

"Rachel?" Prince responded, hearing that his wife was emotional.

"No, it's Aries," she replied, being truthful with him for the first time.

"What? Rachel? What are you talking about?" Prince asked. "You're not making any sense."

"I need you to come here, Prince. I need to explain a lot of things to you . . . come clean about a lot of stuff," she rambled. "I would rather do it face to face. It's not safe there. You have to grab Tre and leave right now. Meet me in Las Vegas. I'll pick you up from McCarran International," Aries said.

"What? Rachel . . . Aries . . . whoever you are. What are you talking about?" Prince asked.

Aries sighed deeply, knowing that to Prince none of this made sense. "Prince, go to the front door and look outside. Have you noticed a new car sitting on the block since I've been gone? Maybe a cable van or a worker from the power company has been lingering around?"

Prince frowned and stood to his feet. "I'll be right back, champ," he said to his son as he picked him up off his lap and put him on the couch. He walked outside and pretended as though he was checking their curbside mailbox as he glanced up the street. A white van sat three houses down from his home.

"There's a van," he said into the phone.

"Go back inside the house," Aries stated. "There are men inside of that van who want to harm you and Tre."

"Rachel, you're talking crazy, like this is something out of a gangster movie," Prince said as he went back inside. Despite the fact that he was unsure, he double-locked the door and pulled the curtains closed.

"This isn't a movie, baby. It's real life. Trust me, I've been living it for years," Aries replied. "Go to the bookshelf in the living room and pull down the encyclopedia and open it up."

Prince did as he was told out of curiosity, and when he opened the book, he saw that the pages had been cut out in the shape of a gun and a 9 mm hand pistol lay inside.

"Rachel! What is this? Why do you have a gun?" Prince asked in shock.

"Because I need one. Listen, baby, I know none of this makes any sense to you right now, but I will explain everything soon. I just need to get you and Tre out of that house," Aries stated. "The gun is loaded, Prince, and a round is already chambered, so be careful. All you have to do is flick the switch on the side of the gun. When you see a red dot, the gun is ready to be fired. Do not hesitate, Prince. If any strangers come to our door, put a hole through them."

"Goodness. You sound like you've done this before!" Prince stated. His heart beat frantically as he began to sweat nervously.

"Come to Vegas, Prince. Don't pack a bag. Get Tre right now and go to the car. You book the first flight out of Barbados, you hear me?" Aries asked.

"Y–y–yeah, I hear you. When I see you, be ready to tell me the truth about who you are, because the woman I'm talking to isn't the same woman I married."

Chapter Twenty

Aries paced back and forth in the busy airport. She had fled L.A. to insure the safety of her family. She had driven to Nevada to meet her husband and son as they disembarked the plane. There was no way that her family would be able to stay on the West Coast, and going back to Barbados was out of the question. She would have to lay low in one of the fifty states. Big city life was no longer an option. She would become such a recluse that only those she reached out to directly would be able to find her.

She watched the large electronic screen that showed arrivals and departures. She smiled when she noticed that the plane carrying her family had arrived safely. She waited anxiously and impatiently, checking her watch every few minutes.

She knew that Prince would ask a thousand questions, but she didn't care. Aries planned to be honest with him about everything. At that moment, she just wanted him to hold her, and she wanted to see her child's smile.

Aries watched as the passengers began to come down to the baggage area, knowing that the two men in her life were lost in the thick crowd. Once the passengers dispersed a bit, she frowned.

"Where is he?" she asked herself aloud as she put her hands on her hips in frustration. She searched the crowd once more before panic set in.

Just as Aries was about to call him, she heard her phone ring. Relief flooded her when she saw Prince's number on her screen.

"Where are you? I'm here waiting for you," Aries asked after she put the cell phone to her ear.

"You're going to be waiting for a long time, bitch."

Aries' stomach went hollow as soon as she heard Case's voice. She had gotten ghost on him, thinking that she could disappear before he found her, but obviously she was wrong.

"Cat got your tongue?" Case asked. "I told you not to fuck with me. Macy Sigel is still breathing, and I don't have my money. Say good-bye to your husband."

"Baby, I love you. I love you. . . . Please, God, no!" she heard Prince yell.

"No . . . wait! Case! Case! We had a deal. I can still find Macy!" she shouted. Bystanders in the airport looked at her as if she were insane.

"Deal is off," Case stated callously. Case had already moved two moves ahead of Aries and met her family before they could get to her.

BOOM!

Aries heard the gunshot and fell to her knees. "Noooooooooo! Prince!"

The line went dead, and Aries gripped the phone tightly in her hand as she sobbed right there in the middle of the curious spectators. Case has just taken everything from her. The world had come crashing down around her, and pure regret filled her heart. Aries was hysterical, and all that could be heard was her shrill screams as airport security helped her from the floor and escorted her away.

***

Six months later

Case puffed a spliff as he watched the young girl go down on him. His toes curled as his dick disappeared and reappeared repeatedly as she devoured him. Life was good in Arizona.

The heat surrounding Macy's disappearance had become too much. He had fled L.A. and switched trades. He was moving weed across the Mexican border now and living in a modest home in a new city. Things were good, and although he wasn't living as plush as he had been in the big city, he was more than comfortable. He had a profitable new hustle going on and had set up a nice new life for himself.

Case closed his eyes and tilted his head back in pure pleasure. "Just like that, ma," he moaned as he ran his hands through her hair.

He was so engrossed in the sexual act that he never heard the bedroom door open. Case had gotten careless since moving out of L.A. He relocated to the desert town in Arizona. He never expected to encounter any problems in the new environment. It wasn't until he felt the girl stop performing fellatio that he opened his eyes.

"Keep going. What you—"

His words were slapped out of his mouth by the barrel of Aries' handgun. Case spit out two of his teeth as he watched the young girl freeze in fear.

"Get your clothes on and leave," Aries stated. "Forget you ever saw me, you understand?"

The girl nodded nervously and grabbed her clothing before leaving at lightning speed from the room while scrambling to get dressed.

Case was frozen. He knew that there was no avoiding this fate, and as he looked down the barrel of her gun, he smirked. There was nothing to say between them. He knew why she had come. He could see the heartbreak in her eyes. She had come for blood, and his was about to be shed.

What Case didn't know was that Aries wanted him to die slowly. She placed the gun directly between his legs and fired.

"Aghh!" Case screamed as his most private of parts exploded. He lunged for her, but pain overtook him and caused his strength to deplete.

He wrestled with Aries, but she was relentless and more cold-blooded than ever. She gripped his shoulder with one hand as she jabbed her gun into his gut with the other.

POP! POP! POP!

Case folded like a lawn chair as lead filled his abdomen.

"Wait. Please, I don't want to die," Case stated as he watched Aries' back as she turned to leave.

Her nostrils flared as she heard his dying words. Aries detested men like Case; they were weak. Case had ended so many lives, ruined so many futures with his reign of terror over L.A.'s streets. Now when it was his time to meet with the Grim Reaper, he was bitching up, begging for mercy.

Aries walked back over to Case and blew his brains out of his head. His body fell limply to the floor as Aries walked away without looking back.

Macy swept the floors of the empty elementary school. It was 3:00 A.M. and he was about to clock out from his second shift job. Macy had come a long way from the lavish life. Because he was such a recognizable political figure it had been hard for him to find a new place to call home. His face had been plastered on the national news for weeks so he was forced into seclusion in the countryside of North Dakota. It was a lonely life, but it was a free life and he would do anything to ensure that it stayed that way. He purchased a small home and maintained it with his janitorial job at the local school. It was a far fall from grace but an adjustment that he was willing to make to maintain control over his own life. Macy wasn't built for the system so running was his only option. He clocked out after a long day's work and drove his Chevy Silverado truck home.

Macy wished that he had someone to come home to. Years of being in love with Fatima had spoiled him. There was nothing like having a wife to tend to his needs and despite all the treachery that had crept into their relationship, he still thought of her from time to time. If he could take back that fateful night that he had murdered Boomer, he would. Their relationship had been solid until he had done the unthinkable. Fatima had meant the world to him and when he heard of her death he had grieved heavily. He had no family, no friends. It was only Macy and the lifetime of regret that he was filled with. Macy was a man seeking redemption, but he had yet to find it, and until he did, he forever felt the empty hole in his chest where his heart used to be.

He put his key in the door and stepped inside. He was greeted by the warm colors of his comfortable living room. Exhausted, he removed his shirt and went into his bathroom. He stood in front of the mirror, noticing his full, scruffy five o'clock shadow. Macy chuckled to himself because he had always been clean cut. The new look appeared odd to him, making him feel like a completely different person.

Macy turned on the water and splashed water on his face. When he came back up, all color left his face at the face in the mirror behind him.

Aries stood unflinchingly cold, with a gun pointed at the back of his head.

"You came after me," he stated as he continued to rub the soap into his beard.

"Because of you I'm a widow," she replied.

"No, because of you you're a widow. You knew the consequences of your actions and you also knew that one day you would meet your match. I'm sorry that you had to experience such pain, but I'm not to blame for it. Case is. He's the one who you should be killing."

Aries pulled back the hammer of the gun.

CLICK!

All she had to do was pull the trigger.

"I did that already."

Macy looked at her in shock, revealing his true emotions to her for the first time.

"Then what is this about?" he asked.

"I always finish the job," she replied.

As he stared into the eyes of a killer, he had no choice but to respect her. She was thorough, and even though she had the power to end his life, he was fascinated by her. He held up his hands in defeat. "I played the game and lost. Now it's time to pay up. Do what you have to do, ma. Just business, right?"

Aries placed her gun directly against Macy's forehead and her trigger finger itched. For the first time in her entire career as a murder-for-hire, she hesitated. She gritted her teeth and ice-grilled Macy as they stared at one another. For some reason, Macy sparked something inside of Aries . . . something good.

"Aghh!" she yelled as she withdrew her weapon. "I'm not going to kill you—today. I can't guarantee that I'll feel this way tomorrow or the next day or the day after that, but today you get to keep your life. As you can see, I can touch you. Anywhere you go, I can get to you. You will live every day thinking if it is the day a Murder Mama is coming for you."

Aries walked out of the house feeling as if she had just taken the first step toward beginning a new life.

Aries hurried into her hotel room and smiled when she saw her son's sleeping face. She was grateful to God for sparing Tre. Although Prince had paid the ultimate price for her sins, her son had been safely tucked away in the panic room before Case ever knew he was home. After everything that she had been through, she had made it through. She looked at the luggage that sat next to the door. She had only come to town to tie up loose ends with Macy, but she no longer felt the need to end more lives. She was pretty sure that she and Macy had an understanding, and that was good enough for her. Enough blood had been shed. The Murder Mamas had taken a lot of wins, but had also experienced some heart-shattering losses.

"We are out of here first thing tomorrow, baby boy. You and I are going to live happily ever after. We have a new life to begin living," she whispered as she admired his innocent face.

As she went to the door, she locked it and then rubbed the tattoo on the back of her wrist. She remembered the day that she and her girls had pledged their allegiance to the game and gotten them inked on. That seemed like so long ago. *Who would've ever thought that I'd be the last one standing?* she thought.

"Beatrice . . . Anisa . . . Miamor . . . Robyn. Rest in peace, Mamas! I love you bitches forever, but it's time to let it go." A single tear slid down her face, because there had been so many good times. She would miss them every day, and because of the lessons they had taught her, she would value every breath that she took. She would live life to the fullest on behalf of them all. "R.I.P., ladies. I'll never forget you."

The Murder Mamas are no more
but . . .
The Cartel 4 is coming.
www.AshleyJaQuavis.com
Follow us on Twitter @Ashleyjaquavis